CROW'S REVENGE

DEVIL'S MURDER MC

USA TODAY BESTSELLING AUTHOR

NIKKI LANDIS

Cover by Pretty in Ink Creations

Models: Matthew Hosea & Jaci Ayers

Image: RplusM Photo

Table of Contents

Author's Note
AUTHOR'S NOTE

AUTHOR'S NOTE

Crow's Revenge is the fifth book in the Devil's Murder MC.

It's filled with dark and gritty content, a supernatural twist, steamy scenes, violence, biker slang, torture, kidnapping, revenge, forced proximity, and a motorcycle club president at war with a ruthless adversary. Mature readers only. Heed the CWs and proceed with caution. Tough subjects occur in this book, please don't read if they will cause you discomfort.

I hope you enjoy the continuing story of Crow, Bella, and the Devil's Murder MC.

The series contains ongoing storylines and themes that may not be resolved in every book, but each couple will eventually receive their HEA. There is a crossover with the Royal Bastards MC where Grim, Rael, Papa, Mammoth, and other members use their reapers to serve justice.

Common Terms

COMMON TERMS

DMMC Devil's Murder Motorcycle Club. One-percenter outlaw MC with several chapters within the U.S. Founded in Henderson, NV 1981.

The Crow Shifter ability & shared soul of every Devil's Murder club member; a black feathered, predatory bird with enhanced traits.

Murder A group of crows, an omen of death.

Kraa An intense cry from a crow, fueled by strong emotion.

The Roost Bar & clubhouse owned by the Devil's Murder MC.

Bull's Saloon Second home to club members, bar owned by Lucky Lou.

Mobbing Individual crows assembling together to harass a rival or predator by cooperatively attacking it.

One-percenter Outlaw biker/club.

Pres President of the club. His orders/decisions are law.

Ol' lady A member's woman, protected wife status.

Cut Leather vest worn by club members, adorned with patches and club colors, sacred to members.

Church An official club meeting, led by president.

Chapel The location for church meetings in the clubhouse.

Prospect Probationary member sponsored by a ranking officer, banned from church until a full patch.

Full Patch A new member approved for membership.

Rook Former president, son of Jackdaw.

Crow Third generation club member, son of Rook, president.

Hog motorcycle

Cage vehicle

Muffler bunny Club girl, also called sweet butt, cut slut.

DDMC Dirty Death MC, rival motorcycle club.

Club Businesses

Jackdaw Security & Bail Bonds, LLC

Rook's Towing & Recovery, LLC

Rook's Pawn & Loans

CROW'S REVENGE

⁘DEVIL'S MURDER MC⁘

For six months, Crow has been consumed with vengeance.

It's become the driving force for nearly every decision in the club ever since his father, the former president Rook, was murdered.

But when the woman he loves is kidnapped, and a vicious, unpredictable enemy takes Bella, he'll have to join forces with unlikely allies.

Nothing will prevent him from rescuing her, even if he must travel into the heart of his enemy's territory and face the beast head-on.

Revenge is served in ways he could never imagine.

What happens when your enemy isn't your enemy?

What if everything Crow believed to be true was a distortion of the facts, twisted to manipulate his father in a game of lies?

The past exposes painful truths when he receives an unexpected visitor. Can he forgive the wrongs that destroyed his parents and nearly ripped his club apart?

Now all the cards are on the table, the hand has been dealt, and Crow will have to win the game before he loses Bella, his club, and his sanity.

Prologue

ROOK

Six months earlier

MY FIST CLOSED AROUND the crumpled piece of paper in my hand—the note delivered by the prospect who stood before me and nervously shuffled his feet.

"Go," I growled, unable to think beyond the message Undertaker had sent me. The cruel reminder that he would never forgive my careless mistake.

Abigail Holmes. An eye for an eye.

One child's life for another.

Fuck!

I couldn't keep my secret any longer. My daughter wasn't safe.

There was only one choice to make. Crow needed to hear the truth. The club would protect Abigail. Even if something happened to me, my son would do the right thing.

1

Not that he was here for me to confide in.

"Why the fuck does he have to be so goddamn stubborn?"

I felt the presence of my crow and his chitter outside as he hopped around, amused by my question.

"Yeah, he's just like his old man. Determined. Headstrong. Nobody can tell him a fuckin' thing. Always got to figure it out himself."

With a sigh, I scrubbed my hand down my face and over my beard, wondering when my son would return home. He'd have to head this way soon, whether he was ready or not. I needed him. Abigail was in danger.

There was only one thing left to do. I had to pay a visit to Howie Baker.

My gaze lowered to the crinkled paper and the words written on it. I snarled as I stomped across the room to my desk, reaching underneath the front drawer to push a hidden button. The latch released with a click, popping open the secret compartment underneath.

Over the years since Abigail's birth, I'd added mementos about her accomplishments. The newspaper clipping from when she won the state spelling bee championship at eight years old. When she won the grand prize in a coloring contest at age ten. Her high school and college graduation photos. Some of the happiest moments of her life, as cherished by me, her Uncle Derek, as they had been to her.

Uncle Derek. Fuck, I hated that she never learned the truth.

I could never admit I was her father. It placed a target on her back. After all these years, I'd been sure I'd done the right thing. None of my club brothers knew I had a second child. I kept her birth a secret, a promise to her mother that I wouldn't bring Abigail into the biker lifestyle.

And now I wondered if that was a colossal mistake. The club knew nothing about her, and with this new threat, there was no one watching her back. What if Undertaker got to her first?

Fuck!

I shoved all the memorabilia back in the compartment, adding the crumpled note and shutting it with enough force that I heard the lock engage again. Someday, Crow would find this drawer, and maybe he'd understand why I kept his sister a secret. I hoped he could forgive me for the deception.

Abigail? I had no idea how she would react to the truth. Would she despise me for all the years I visited and took her on trips to the zoo and the movies without ever revealing why I loved and spoiled her?

Life had been hard on her despite my best intentions. She had a lazy mother and a worthless piece of shit for a stepfather. When I found out he verbally abused her, I showed up at his job and broke every finger in his right hand. He left her alone after that. But it didn't change the fact that I wondered if I'd made a mistake. Would she have been happier and safer with me and her brother?

I'd never know the answer to that.

There wasn't time to dwell on it. I needed to leave and ensure my daughter wouldn't become prey to a monster. And I had to go alone.

That would pose a big fucking problem because the president of a notorious biker club never went anywhere without backup. Raven, my V.P., and Hawk, my S.A.A., would try to stop me.

I snatched up my keys, wallet, and smokes, shoving everything into my pockets. For this to work, I needed to leave as quickly as possible. A sense of urgency pulsed through me, and I rushed from my room, taking the stairs two at a time until I reached the bottom.

As soon as I finished the meeting with Howie Baker, I'd ride to Abigail's house and tell her everything. With any luck, she'd listen and follow me back to the clubhouse, where I'd introduce my daughter and hold church, asking for a vote to protect her from Undertaker and the Dirty Death MC.

It wasn't a great fucking plan, but it was a plan.

My ass had barely met the saddle of my Harley when a rough voice caught my attention.

"Where are we headed, pres?"

I turned my head, staring at Raven. My best fucking friend. I'd kept my secrets from him, too.

"I need to ride out alone."

"Not gonna happen." His arms crossed over his chest as he frowned. "Something is up. My crow is agitated. Tell me what's going on."

"I received a note," I admitted.

"A fucking note?"

"A threat," I clarified.

His brows shot upward in surprise. "Who? What the fuck do they want?"

"They don't want anything. At least, nothing I can offer."

That was the fucking truth. None of my children would be pawns in Undertaker's sick games.

"Where are you going, pres? Riding out alone won't solve shit. Let me come with you."

I shook my head.

"Then, Hawk. Or Talon. Shit, take Cuckoo or Carrion."

I snorted. "No. I've got to do this alone. It's fucking crucial."

Raven's arms dropped. "Rook," he pleaded, using my road name. He rarely did that.

It hit me in the chest like a punch to the heart. Should I send him to retrieve Abigail? No. She had to hear the truth from me first. I fucked this up enough without adding more shit to the pile.

"There's no other choice." None that I could see. "I'll be back in a few hours."

He swallowed. I didn't think he'd give up so fast, and he didn't. "How about I ride in the distance? Keep watch in case shit goes down. No one has to know, but it'll make me feel a hell of a lot better."

I couldn't do that. Not yet.

"No," I growled. "Not this time."

A panicked look briefly crossed his features. "This doesn't feel right."

He wasn't wrong. None of this was fucking right from the beginning, and the blame originated from me. One stupid, reckless night. Too much liquor. Not enough caution.

I never saw Fang until he ran the red light at 2 a.m. Drunk, I didn't have the reflexes or the clarity to stop or swerve my bike. We collided on the dark asphalt.

Fang was thrown from his bike and hit a pole, crushing his skull on impact. He didn't suffer. But that didn't matter to Undertaker. From the moment of his only son's death, he blamed me. Swore vengeance. I waited every day for the last fifteen years for him to come.

He never had.

I'd often wondered why he let me and my son live. Why wait all this time for revenge?

It wasn't until I saw the property taxes on his land that I thought of a bargain to end our feud. I'd paid them before he could, claiming the deed and stashing it away at The Roost.

That was my ace. Undertaker didn't own his property anymore or the clubhouse for the Dirty Death MC. I did.

But I didn't want to keep it. This was my chance to secure Abigail and Crow's safety. I wouldn't sell it. Just a trade. The deed for their lives. Seemed reasonable to me. Undertaker only won in this deal. I hoped he would see it that way.

"It's got to be this way. Trust me."

Raven dipped his chin. "Okay, pres."

"I'll be back in a few hours, probably not alone."

That caught his attention. "Who's comin'?"

"I need you to promise me you'll keep this secret."

Raven blinked. "I will."

"Someone who can change the past and heal the club. It'll end the shit with Undertaker and the Dirty Death."

"Damn."

"Be ready for anything," I cautioned.

"I will. Ride safe, brother."

Club brother. Best friend. Family. If something happened to me, Raven would ensure Crow took the throne. He'd help run the club and keep it moving forward. I trusted him because he was blood to me.

"If shit goes south, make sure Crow comes home and takes the president patch."

Raven flinched. "Fuck, Rook. Now I need to come with you."

"No, It's got to be this way. There are too many lives at risk. You've got to follow orders."

His face flushed, and I knew Raven was pissed.

"Don't follow me. I'm not asking as your pres. I'm asking as your best fucking friend and brother. Let me do this."

Defeat settled over his features. "Alright. You have my word."

His word was resolute. If Raven gave it, he'd never betray it.

"I need to ride. Now."

I left the parking lot outside The Roost and never looked back. I couldn't bear the thought of seeing Raven's face or any of the club members when I left them behind. It hurt, and my chest ached. For the first time in over forty years, I put my children first and the club second—a choice I should have made long ago.

Fuck. It was another item on a long list of regrets.

Losing Crow's mother because of this life. Choosing the club over Abigail's mother. Letting the past rip me apart from the only woman I ever truly loved, Crow's mother, Laurel. The rift between me and my son because I held on too fucking tight. Not being there enough for my daughter. They eroded my composure as I gripped the handlebars on my bike and sped toward Bakers' Law Offices.

I parked my bike in the front spot, loading my helmet inside my saddlebags before I trudged up the steps and entered the building.

The receptionist greeted me with a smile. "Hello. Do you have an appointment?"

"Don't need one," I muttered, heading toward Howie Baker's door.

"Hey, you can't barge in there!"

"Honey, I can do whatever the fuck I want."

Pink dusted her cheeks.

I turned the knob and entered Howie's office. "It's time," I announced.

Howie shot to his feet as his secretary rushed inside. "It's fine. Cancel my appointments for the rest of the day. This is urgent, Sally."

She gave him a funny look and nodded, shutting the door behind her as she left.

"I wondered when I'd see you again," Howie began, opening his desk drawer to pull out a bottle of whiskey and two glasses. He filled them both and pushed one in my direction.

I took the drink, tossed back its contents, and enjoyed the resulting burn. "I need the documents."

He paused with the glass halfway to his mouth. "Shit."

Yeah, shit. "I got a note this morning."

"He found your daughter."

It didn't surprise me that Howie reached that conclusion without a nudge from me. "Yes."

"Then we need to secure our investments and put the plan in place."

"Already done on my end. I spoke to Raven. The club will know what to do. I need the envelope mailed to the clubhouse right away, addressed to Crow. I'm going to pick up my daughter when I leave here."

"Done." Howie drained his glass and placed it on his desk. "I'll leave first. Close up my office and send Sally on her way. I don't want her caught in the middle as collateral damage if Undertaker had you followed."

I already considered that option. But since he enjoyed toying with me, I didn't think he'd make a move yet. He wanted me to squirm first, like the worm dangling from a hook above the gaping mouth of a fish.

"He won't. Not yet."

"I hope you're right." Howie cleared his throat. "He can't know my role in this."

"As far as I know, he doesn't. That's why I made sure no one followed me here. Took a couple of detours on the way."

Howie nodded. Relief swept over his features. "Good." He stood and walked to a framed picture on his wall, plucking it away and placing it on the ground by his feet. A safe had been concealed. He spun the dial for the combination before opening it. "Here." He reached inside and pulled out an envelope, handing it over. "Check that it's in order before I mail it."

I flipped through the contents, skimming the documents inside. Crow's birth certificate. Abigail's birth certificate. My marriage license with Crow's mother, Laurel. Her forged death certificate I promised to hold, breaking Laurel's connection to the world she'd grown to hate. It was all here.

"It's complete."

"Then I'll prepare the package."

Howie addressed the envelope and sealed it, placing it inside his open briefcase. He'd popped it onto his desk while I checked all the documents. Inside, he added cash, passports, and other items that weren't my business. The safe had been emptied.

He left it open. There was nothing left to conceal.

"Do you still have the letter for Laurel?"

"Yes."

"Mail that too."

How pursed his lips. "As you wish."

I glanced at my phone, swiping to open it, sending funds from my account. "Your final payment has been made."

Howie shut his briefcase and locked it. "I won't be reachable until this is finished."

"I understand."

We both walked toward his door.

Howie turned to me. "I hope it works out. Abigail should be at The Roost with you and Crow. It's her legacy."

"Yes," I agreed. My legacy, passed on to both of my children.

I watched as he gave instructions to Sally and told her to take the side entrance and leave. She rushed from us, confusion and fear warring for dominance in her pale blue eyes.

Howie held out his hand. "Best of luck, Austin Derek Holmes. I hope we see each other again someday."

"Under entirely different circumstances," I joked.

"Agreed."

I waited until I heard his car pull away and leave the lot. He didn't take his fancy Mercedes but a second vehicle registered to his mistress. Smart. Howie always covered his tracks well, which was one of the reasons I used his services.

The club had a lawyer on retainer. We used Gil Thomas, and he was worth every cent. He'd helped us on numerous occasions. If I had any other option, I would have obtained Gil's skills for the documents Howie had procured for me, but the need for secrecy trumped my loyalty to Gil.

After checking the windows, I left the quiet office, ensuring no one lingered outside. The property seemed deserted as I sat on my bike. Pulling on my gloves, I started the engine and eased her out of the parking spot, turning toward the road.

The rumble of multiple bike engines alerted me to trouble before I could rise off the seat or head back inside. When I saw the Dirty Death MC cuts, I knew Undertaker must have followed me. But how? I had used every trick I knew to evade him.

My crow swirled above my head, circling the area as he cawed at the men who approached. I sensed his apprehension and concern. I'd come alone against the advice of my V.P. My club would be pissed.

Undertaker, his V.P. Chronos, and several other members blocked my exit as they pulled in, forming a row of six bikes. I wondered how they found me. I left no trail. I'd made sure no one followed. How was this fucking possible? And what did the asshole want? To threaten me again?

I opened my mouth to speak when the strangest scent caught me unaware. A smell that resembled decay and something sinister. Above my head, my crow rattled his throat. *Kraaa!*

Undertaker's grin spread wide as our eyes met. "Yes. You sense it. Good."

What the fuck was he? And his club? Fucking *wolves*? How the hell did we miss this? How did they conceal it?

"You should know I'm no ordinary Alpha. The vargulf has taken leadership over my pack." He pulled a gun, aiming at my heart. "I want to rip you apart and feast on your organs. I need you to feel the same pain I felt when you killed Fang."

There would never be anything I could do to make that right.

Chronos and the other DDMC snarled, growling at Undertaker's words. I'd stolen a life. Taken the Alpha's son from his father and the pack. I deserved to die for my crime, no matter if it was an accident or not.

"You'll know the agony I feel when your children die by my hand. I will slowly bleed them out as I let the vargulf consume them."

No!

"But you won't be here to witness it."

I blinked as Undertaker ticked his chin at Chronos.

There was nowhere to run, and I wasn't a coward. I'd die like a fucking man on my bike. But it would suck for my kids. Gunned down in the middle of the afternoon. Not a witness to see what happened. My last breaths on this earth leaving my chest with worry and regret.

Chronos reached inside his cut and grabbed his gun. The barrel pointed at my chest. I kept my eyes open, staring my enemy down as he pulled on the trigger. In defiance, I lifted my chin higher and went for my weapon.

It was a futile effort.

I never counted how many bullets it took to knock me from my Harley—more than three. I jolted with every impact. Dark red blood oozed from the wounds as my back met the asphalt. Strangely, I didn't feel much pain.

Maybe I was in shock.

Undertaker laughed as my crow lost his shit, attacking the vargulf. He shredded the skin on the left side of Undertaker's face before taking to the sky, cawing loudly. More crows joined him as they assembled for a mobbing.

Engines thundered as the group left the parking lot, and I heard sirens. Help would never arrive in time.

I felt my essence fading and the crow's panicked chortle. Our bond would sever, and he would be forced to fly alone until his last breath, never bonding to another member of my club.

"I'm sorry," I managed to choke as I sputtered on my lifeblood. "Crow. Abigail."

I promised Laurel if she took on a new identity and left Nevada, I would keep our son safe. I'd break that vow with my death. Crow would be too vulnerable, heartbroken, and furious. He'd want retribution. That was just want Undertaker wanted.

With my murder, my son would be forced to hunt down the Dirty Death MC and kill every last one of them. The club, my children, Laurel, and the crows would never find peace as long as the vargulf and his pack hunted on our land.

My eyes closed, and my body relaxed, the ground beneath my cut saturated with blood as I felt the hot, sticky fluid reach my hair. In those last moments, I thought only of the three people I loved most. My son and daughter. My Laurel.

I hoped they could forgive me.

Chapter 1

CROW

Present day

"FUCK, BELLA. JUST LIKE that," I groaned, my fingers gripping her waist tighter as she rolled her hips, snapping them forward and forcing me deeper inside her. "You keep fucking me like this, and I'm not gonna last long."

"Then you'll just have to make it up to me," she announced as her hands lifted, skimming over her breasts and up into her hair, where she gathered the sweaty strands. Her gaze focused on the mirror anchored to the ceiling. We installed it last week. "Harder, baby."

I loved it when she used that sexy, husky tone. Loved it even more when she clenched her core like she was doing now. My cock got the tightest hug from her pussy.

Her back arched, pushing out her perfect tits as she rode me faster. "More."

1

"You move those hips like a fucking porn star, my queen. Blows my goddamn mind," I growled.

"How about when I do this?"

She reached behind her, leaning backward until her fingers slid around my balls, giving them a gentle squeeze. The added pressure felt too fucking good.

"Gonna be the death of me, babe," I joked.

Bella released my nuts, dragging her nails over my skin. She moved her hand forward again, gripping my cock as she leaned closer to my chest, holding onto the base as I lifted off the mattress to give her every inch of me. "You're so thick. I love it."

"All for you." I slid my palms over the generous swells of her ass and up her back, hooking my hands on her shoulders. At this angle, I could bring her down on my cock and bury deep with each thrust.

"Oh, fuck. That's perfect."

Yeah, it fucking never got old with my ol' lady.

"Gonna come for me yet?" I asked as my lips lingered close to hers, the heat of our breath mingling.

"I'm so close."

"Then let me tip you over the edge," I murmured with a hard tug, knowing I hit the right spot. I felt it.

Bella gasped, slipping her hand between her legs to press on her clit. She circled it once. Twice. And then. . .she fell apart.

Her lips opened, and sounds of pure bliss emptied into the air. "Austin!"

This was my favorite way to end the day. Feeling her spasm around my dick and crying out my name. I slowly pumped my hips, drawing out her orgasm until she fell limp on my chest.

I turned us, laying her back against the mattress while keeping a consistent pace. It didn't take long for me to join her, shuddering as I spilled into my woman.

I kept eye contact as we separated, resting on my back. She joined me as I held out my hand. It was her favorite, cuddling after sex, and I kissed her forehead as she draped over my chest.

"You forgot something important, you know."

I did? "Enlighten me, beautiful."

She lifted her head and rested her chin on her hands, staring into my eyes. "It's our six-month anniversary."

I blinked. Huh?

"Since the night of our first date at Hoover Dam," she clarified.

Well, fuck. I did forget. "I'll make it up to you, Bella, mine."

"I know you will. That's why I already bought my present from you. It's gorgeous. Thank you."

A laugh bubbled up my chest and out of my mouth as I sat up, kissing her sweet, plump lips. She always tasted like bubblegum and cotton candy—her favorite lip gloss flavor.

"So feisty," I teased.

"Do you want your gift now?"

"Abso*fucking*lutely."

She slid from the mattress, shaking her ass on the way to the bathroom. "Me on my knees. You naked in the shower. How does that sound?"

I scrambled from the bed, chasing her inside as she jumped into the stall, turning on the water. Once it was warm, we both stood under the spray, letting the hot water sluice over us.

Bella lowered to her knees, giving me that fuck-me grin that I loved. When her hand wrapped around the base of my cock, I groaned with need. When her lips covered the head and sucked, I had to slap my hand against the tiled wall to remain upright. She swallowed me down, and I swore to fuck I would marry this woman and make her mine before the end of the year.

Later, when we both left our apartment on the third floor of the clubhouse, I held her hand. We needed food, and I led her to the chow hall, admiring the long row of silver pans and the candles under them, keeping everything warm. I was fucking starving. Bella filled her plate as I piled food onto two, noting the secret smile lingering on her lips.

"It's your fault."

"Oh? How's that?" She snagged a breakfast potato from my plate and popped it in her mouth.

"You have a perfect pussy."

She tilted her head to the side. "And my mouth?"

"Goddamn heaven on earth."

She snickered. "That's why I stick around, Crow. You need me."

"Every fucking day," I replied without humor. I was serious. "You're my forever, Bella, mine."

She loved the cheesy shit I said to her, but I meant every word. Some couples didn't banter the way we did, but I loved that my ol' lady was unpredictable. She kept me on my toes, my dick happy, and my heart fucking full.

"You're my ride-or-die and my forever, too." She popped a kiss on my lips before stealing another potato off my plate.

"Babe, would you like some potatoes?"

"Honey, why do I need my own when you have that big pile on yours?"

Soft laughter caught my attention, and I turned to see my sister. *My sister.* It still didn't seem real that she was here. Gail stood with Talon, scooping scrambled eggs onto her plate.

"Morning, Nightingale," I greeted her, using the nickname our father had given her, but I'd also called her without knowing about it.

"Morning, big brother."

Talon ticked his chin my way. "Hey, pres."

"Talon."

Yeah, I was still pissed at him. He was supposed to protect my sister, not fuck her. And now she was in love with him. My fucking enforcer. An outlaw biker. I wanted a better life for her than that. My pops did. He kept her out of this life to keep her safe. *Fuck.*

Bella's hand rested on my arm. "It's what she wants," she whispered, reminding me I had no control over this.

"Let's eat."

Yeah, now I was in a mood with the reminder, which only brought all the other shit I had to handle back into focus. I tried to brush it aside for Bella while we ate breakfast, but I knew she could tell I was preoccupied.

I tugged her close for a kiss after we finished and cleared our dishes from the table. "Gotta talk to my officers, babe."

"Have fun. I'm going to bake with Bree and set up the teapot for my afternoon with Gail."

"She loves your teatime. I asked her."

"I do, too."

I loved that my ol' lady and my sister were becoming best friends. Made my life a hell of a lot easier having them both in the same place and protected. "You're so fuckin' sweet, Bella. I can't get enough of that sugar."

"You will later."

"Yeah, I will." I slapped her on the ass. "Meet you at our room for dinner."

"It's a date."

Raven, Hawk, and Talon were already seated around the table in the chapel when I entered. Lucky Lou nearly bumped into my ankles with his new scooter when I started to close the door.

"Hold on. I got shit to say."

"Don't let me hold you back," I grunted as he nearly clipped the side of the table.

Raven coughed to hide his laugh. Hawk sipped from a fresh beer. And Talon? He didn't react, watching me enter the room and take my seat at the head of the table.

This wasn't church. I didn't slam the gavel down. When I met with my officers, it was less formal.

"I'm gonna give the floor to Lou first," I announced, snagging one of the beers from the center.

"Mighty gracious of you," he acknowledged. "I want to look at those documents Rook sent to you again. Got 'em handy, Crow?"

I did. There was a safe in this room, and I occasionally kept paperwork that I didn't stash in my office. "In the safe. Give me a minute."

I set down my beer and pushed away from the table, walking to the safe to open it. The design was clever. If you didn't know what you were looking for, you'd never find the location. I'd hidden it within the interior of the bar's wooden base. The only way to open it was to move a specific stack of glasses out of the way. I spun the dial and worked the combination, popping the door open. Once I had the envelope I needed, I returned to my seat.

Lou reached for the documents as I handed them over. "That's right," he murmured, as if he had forgotten what was inside.

I will never forget. There was my birth certificate. Gail's birth certificate. The marriage license between my father and my mother, Laurel Holmes. And a death certificate for Laurel.

Until I received that envelope, I didn't know that she died. Rook never told me. My pops could be far too secretive, and this added another on top of the pile I would never learn about. My mother left me when I was a kid and nearly ruined my life.

6

If I hadn't had such a devoted father and men like Raven and Lucky Lou to bring me up right, I would have been a lost cause. I battled anger, abandonment issues, and the painful realization that I wasn't enough reason for my mother to stick around or take me with her. To this day, I still didn't know why she left and turned her back on us. Was it the club? Something my father did?

"It wasn't your fault."

My gaze flicked to Lou. "It felt like it back then."

"But it wasn't. Sometimes people can't work through their shit. It's fucked but the truth."

Yeah, I knew that now. Tell it to my inner seven-year-old.

"This death certificate of your mother's. It's strange."

"Strange?" Hawk asked.

"Yeah. It says the cause of death was Diabetes. That's wrong."

"What?"

"He's right," Raven agreed. "Laurel wasn't diabetic."

Raven would know. Of course, health conditions can change with time.

"Maybe it developed later."

"That's the thing that's odd about this certificate," Lou continued, "It's her weight. It's fucking high. Nearly three hundred pounds."

Raven frowned. "Laurel was always slender."

Lou pointed to a spot on the certificate. "Says she didn't have any edema. A1C was low."

I scrubbed a hand down my face, trying not to get agitated by this. What did it matter now? "Lou."

"This is important, Crow. You got to hear it. I don't think your mama is dead."

"Well, shit," Hawk blurted.

Wow. "You think it's fake? Why the fuck for?"

"To keep her safe," Talon answered. "It makes sense, pres. Rook protected your sister and kept her hidden. It's not farfetched to think he would have done the same for the woman he loved."

I shoved away from the table, pacing the floor. Could I have been wrong? Did my mother leave because she didn't have a choice? Was she threatened? Did Undertaker and the Dirty Death MC go after Laurel? "Fuck."

Lou placed the documents back in the envelope and slid it my way. "Yeah, fuck. We need to investigate this."

"It could be nothing," Hawk pointed out.

"Or we could find someone who isn't supposed to be found," Talon added. "If this is true, Rook and Laurel had their reasons for keeping these secrets."

Raven leaned forward, placing his elbows on the table. "This is all a guess. We don't know shit. I don't like being in the dark, pres. If Undertaker or the Dirty Death have any chance of having a hand in this, we need to check it out."

Lou nodded, pounding his fist on the table. "That's what I'm saying."

"I don't even know where to start," I admitted. "I've got no information about Laurel."

"With Eagle Eye. He can do a deep dive. Find out everything he can on the internet about Laurel."

"That's a start, Hawk."

Lou tapped the table. "She had two sisters. They might still be alive. It's a good lead to follow up on while waiting for Eagle Eye."

"Then I'll go talk to him now. This stays with us. It doesn't leave this room."

Four heads nodded.

I left the chapel, ignoring the sudden churning in my gut.

Could my mother still be alive?

Chapter 2

BELLA

"I'M SO GLAD WE have our own table," I observed, taking the seat across from Gail. It had become a routine for us every afternoon—a few minutes of relaxation and girl time. I placed a dark pink floral tablecloth over a square table in the corner and added a pretty crystal vase with fresh flowers.

The guys avoided it, mostly because I had also put a giant sign up. In case any of the club members forgot, the easel would remind them.

Gail giggled when she glanced at it. "You changed the message."

"I sure the fuck did." I shrugged. "If they want to risk it, it's on them. I *will* get stabby. This is our spot."

I'd drawn a big fat cock on the chalkboard, then an equal sign, followed by a knife dripping blood all in colored chalk. I dared any of the Devil's Murder to try to sit at this table—even the president. Only ol' ladies allowed.

1

"It is," she agreed, reaching for a cinnamon roll. "Bree's baked goods are my favorite. I'm going to get fat eating all the wonderful food she cooks."

"You're not kidding. I keep telling my sister she needs to open that bakery she's been dreaming about."

"I don't know Bree well enough yet, but I'll keep trying to convince her too."

Crow brought Gail to The Roost, the Devil's Murder clubhouse only a week prior. I met her in the middle of the night, thrilled to finally connect with the young woman who was the only living blood relative of the guy I loved.

To get to know her, I set up tea the following afternoon, and it quickly became a special time for me. I hoped she felt the same. Gail reminded me so much of her brother. She had the same gray eyes and smile, an ability to command a room when they entered it, and even the same walk that bordered on a strut.

Crow's presence was powerful. Magnetic.

Gail was the softer but no less charismatic equal.

She sighed as she stirred honey into her tea. "Austin's still mad at Talon."

"Yeah, honey, I think so. It's gonna take time. Your brother is overprotective of the ones he loves. But you? Finding out he has a sister after all this time? He's thrilled but also scared he'll lose you."

"I guess I can understand that."

Did I mention they were both stubborn? Almost to a fault?

"He's known too much loss," she observed.

"First, his mom. Then Rook. It's been a lot to handle."

"And now I'm here, and it's all chaos."

"But none of that is your fault."

"I try to tell myself that."

"You had no idea about the club, Rook's death, your brother, or the war with the Dirty Death MC until a few weeks ago. I'm sure you're just as overwhelmed," I pointed out.

"I am. But you, Talon, and my brother are helping me through this. I'm glad Crow has you in his life. You're good for him, Bella."

"Thanks. That means a lot, Gail."

"I may be learning a lot about my brother, but I see the way he looks at you. You soften him in the best ways. He can be an ass," she joked.

"You have no idea. That man is like a bull, all charge and rage when he's pissed or threatened." I took a sip of my tea. "One of the things that I love about him is how fiercely he protects and cares about those around him."

"He's a good man. Like Rook." Her expression grew wistful. "I wonder what it would have been like to grow up around the club? Probably crazy."

"Oh, yeah. He's told me stories," I laughed. "I'm surprised he made it to adulthood with some of the shit he's pulled."

She smirked at that. "I can imagine." Gail cleared her throat and set down her mug. "I've been meaning to ask you something."

"Okay. Go for it."

"Are you planning to marry my brother? Because I don't think he could survive without you."

That wasn't what I expected her to ask at all. I blinked, and then we both dissolved into giggles.

"Damn straight. He lost his wallet this morning, and I found it on the bathroom sink. I'd blame all the products I have as a distraction, but he's the one who bought all the lotion, hair care, and skin cream."

Gail snickered. "He spoils you like Talon spoils me."

"Yes," I agreed. "Talon would raise hell on earth for you. I've never seen him so affectionate and protective. Funny how we bring out a different side to these men when they fall for us."

"Yeah. It's sweet."

"Who's sweet? You both talkin' about me?"

We both turned to see Cuckoo approaching us, stopping when he reached the table. I still wasn't used to his crazy costumes. Every time I saw him, he wore something different. The guy must have dozens of totes full of props, masks, and clothing. I bet his room was a nightmare.

My gaze slid over him, taking in his newest creation. He wore a black striped prisoner shirt and pants. The sleeves had been ripped off, and Cuckoo's arms were bare, showing off his dark ink, biceps, and muscled forearms. A prisoner's number in black block letters stretched over his chest. He wore his cut over the shirt. It sort of worked in an odd way. The bottom of his pants was loosely tucked into black boots.

A chain hung from his belt loop, and he'd attached several shrunken head props. One mouth gaped in a silent scream. His face was painted with Halloween makeup like a demented clown with blood splatter on the cheeks and forehead. He finished off the look with a headband that appeared to show a knife through his skull. Handle on the left and the end of the blade on the right. It wasn't a cheap one either. Almost looked real.

He grinned as we stared, exposing bright white vampire teeth. It seemed to be a favorite item. He wore them often.

"You do attract attention," I murmured.

He wiggled his brows. "In more ways than one."

Gail tilted her head, tapping her chin with a long, manicured nail. "I believe that's the best costume I've ever seen."

He slapped a hand over his heart. "Gail Holmes. You just made my heart melt."

She snorted. I rolled my eyes.

4

"I think you should ditch Talon and ride with me, darlin'."

"I think he'd probably kick your ass if he ever heard you say that," Gail laughed.

Cuckoo seemed to think it over. "Damn. It's tempting to see if he'd try."

I shooed him away from the table. "Scoot. You're interrupting girl time."

Cuckoo reached for a cinnamon roll, and I swatted at his hand, too late to prevent the theft. He winked as he backed away, taking a massive bite.

"You're an ass, Cuckoo!" I shouted, gaining a few chuckles from the guys around us.

Gail shook her head. "He's a handful."

"You just wait until he meets his mate. I'm going to have so much fun."

"We both will."

Later that afternoon, I stuck my head in the kitchen, looking for my sister. Two club girls were cutting up veggies and boiling pasta. They split the chores, including cleaning, cooking, and shopping, although their primary duty involved pleasing the members, specifically the single guys in the club.

Since my arrival, I hadn't seen anyone cheat and hoped I didn't. I didn't think I'd be able to keep my mouth shut, and that could cause trouble. For now, I didn't dwell on it.

"Anyone see Bree?"

"She's outside at the picnic tables."

Of course. I should have checked there first. "Thanks."

I found Bree in the shade, sipping on lemonade. Her long hair was piled high on her head in a messy bun due to the scorching temperature outdoors. This summer had already reached record highs. I joined her, taking the empty lounge chair on her right.

To her left, Lucky Lou sat in his new red scooter. They weren't talking, but I noticed they enjoyed the solitude on numerous occasions. It wasn't the first time Lou sat with her outdoors or in the kitchen while she baked. They shared a connection, one that Bree needed after all the trauma she'd endured.

Lou was a kind, patient, and cantankerous older man who liked to shake things up a bit when he visited. The only exception to that was his visits with Bree. He knew what she needed to heal, and he gave his time, support, and unflinching aid to her recovery.

"The breeze is cooler than yesterday," I announced, crossing my feet at the ankles. "It's risen from the lower levels of hell to the highest tier of hell."

Lou snickered.

Bree's lips quivered with amusement. "I think you're right."

"That means we need more lemonade. I'll go rustle us up some." He winked before pulling back on the lever with his hand, prompting his scooter to creep toward the entrance to the clubhouse.

"Those cinnamon rolls were to die for this morning. It's the best batch you've made to date."

"Thanks. I added a little more vanilla to the dough."

"They were perfect."

She turned her head, catching my gaze. "I know what you're doing. I'm okay, Bell. Really. It gets better every day." Her hand lowered, and she rubbed her growing belly. "This baby doesn't know how he was conceived, and it doesn't matter. He'll know love and grow up with two parents that would do anything for him."

I didn't know if I could do it. How the hell did you keep a baby after rape? "He'll have wonderful parents. Raven already loves him."

She smiled, laying her head back. "I want to start that bakery, but I don't know how I'd get it going with the pregnancy."

"Well," I began, swinging my legs over the chair and resting my feet on the ground, "I've got an idea who your partner should be. She's got fantastic taste and small business experience. You should seriously talk to her about it."

Bree laughed. "Well, sis, I thought that was what we're doing. You sell jewelry. I'll sell all the yummy treats."

"We can call it Bling & Bake!" I exclaimed.

"Uh, no." She snorted. "That's awful. It sounds like an edible shop."

Damn. It did.

"What about Buttery Baubles?"

"Sis, we need to work on this."

"Yeah, you're right."

Chapter 3

CROW

T HE CONVERSATION ABOUT LAUREL'S death certificate sparked a new interest in checking my father's office and his desk. It had become mine with his death, but I hadn't yet gone through it. I couldn't until now. Everything was still so fresh and painful. It fucking hurt to open his drawers and look through his shit.

But I had to move beyond that now. There were too many fucking questions that needed answers. Too many things that didn't add up. The more I thought about it, the more I wondered why my father didn't fight harder to keep Laurel with us. What if everything I believed up to now had been a lie?

Jesus. Christ. The truth could change everything.

For over an hour, I dug through his drawers and personal items, notebooks, maps, and junk. A carton of Marlboro Reds. His favorite steel lighter with the club's logo etched onto the front. A few drawings I made of motorcycles in middle school that I didn't know he kept. Awards I'd earned.

A small envelope of photos that included old snapshots of club members like Raven. Damn, he looked young.

On the bottom, I found a picture of my dad, Laurel, and me when I was less than a year old. My pops held me, and his free arm hugged Laurel close against his side. They looked happy. More than that, I caught the way she stared at him like he was everything to her. What the fuck happened to drive them apart?

I sat back in the leather chair my father loved, kicking out my legs. My knee bumped into the underside of his desk, and I heard a click. A latch released with a click, popping open to reveal the secret compartment underneath.

I sat the photographs in my hands to the side, reaching into the compartment to pull out a stack of documents, newspaper clippings, photos, and other memorabilia. All of it was about my sister Gail. He'd kept track of her since her birth, proudly storing away everything he could about his daughter.

I couldn't imagine how hard it would be to keep my child a secret and love her from a distance. Rook never showed weakness or vulnerability. That was part of his position as the president of a 1 %er motorcycle club. But as I thought about it, I remembered moments when he would seem too distant or short-tempered. It didn't happen often. I wondered if Gail or my mother was the reason.

These items had to have been precious to my father. In our house, pictures of me, my pops, and his club had been displayed everywhere, but with notable absence, my sister and mother were not. I wish Rook was here to ask. I would have understood if he told me the truth. I'd always wanted a sibling.

A sigh escaped as I replaced the memories in the compartment and shut it. A soft click followed. Someday, I'd bring Gail up here and show her what our father had saved. If there wasn't so much shit going down with Undertaker and the Dirty Death, I'd do it now.

But the club and its problems trumped that reveal.

The trip down memory lane led me back to my mother. That seemed to be happening a lot today. I wondered if Eagle Eye had found anything yet. He was fucking fast when it came to this shit. He knew how to search for things I would never think to consider, and he was damn good at getting past firewalls and breaching security. He tapped into government sites all the time without getting caught.

The man was a tech genius.

I found him in his room, staring at two screens and shifting back and forth between them as he keyed in info, brought up flies, switched between them, and moved to the next item. Gave me a damn headache just to watch. The door had been ajar, and I walked in, standing behind him and not wanting to interrupt until he acknowledged me. I knew better than to distract him when he was fishing like this.

"Got an update for you, pres."

Yep. I figured. "Fill me in."

"Laurel left when you were seven, right?"

"Yeah," I confirmed.

"She's been gone nineteen years. People's lives change. They move on. Pop out kids. Advance in their career. Shit like that. But they don't fall off the face of the earth and disappear."

"What's that mean, Eagle Eye?"

"This shit happens when they enter WITSEC."

Witness Protection. "Are you saying the feds got to her?"

Eagle Eye shrugged. "Can't say for sure until I dig a little more, but I can tell you she's a ghost. There isn't shit about Laurel Holmes since she left your pops. Everything is erased. Gone."

"Or never existed because she was given a new identity."

"Exactly."

Goddamn. What the fuck did my mother get involved in?

Why did Rook keep that secret?

"Keep digging."

"I will, pres. I'll text when I have anything else."

"Good."

I left him to work his magic and headed straight to the bar. My ass landed on a stool, and a whiskey appeared in front of me. I thanked the prospect and picked up the shot, downing it in one swallow. "Leave the bottle, Red."

"Sure, pres."

Funny how everything surfaces in your mind when you have a few minutes of silence. The bar was quiet and nearly empty. Most of my guys were working for our various businesses and earned their honest wages that way. Kept the place almost tomb-like during a weekday afternoon.

But Raven and Lucky Lou were always around.

My V.P. took a seat on my right, asking for a beer. He turned my way, lifting his chin. "You got shit on your mind."

I never could hide anything from him. Never wanted to do it either. His guidance meant the world to me, and I respected him as much as my old man. "Too much shit," I admitted. "You'll never guess what I found in Rook's desk."

"A bottle of Macallan."

"Shit," I laughed. "If he had that, we'd be drinking it right now, toasting to him."

"You bet we would." A deep chuckle rumbled up his chest. "What did you find?"

"A hidden compartment full of memories about Gail. Awards. Photos. Newspaper articles. I even found an old shot of you and Rook. You've gotten old, Raven."

"Asshole." He smirked. "Damn. Now that we know about Gail, it doesn't surprise me. Kind of makes my heart ache for him a little, ya know?"

I did. "Yeah."

"That was a hell of a burden to carry alone."

"He chose it that way," I replied, unable to hide a slight bitterness from my tone. "He should have trusted us, Raven. Me and you and Lucky Lou. We always had his back."

"I know, Crow. I'm sorry." He gripped my shoulder. "It's not easy to learn all this shit. It's a lot to deal with on top of his death."

"His murder," I clarified.

"Ain't a soul disputing that, pres."

Fuck. "This shit has me all twisted."

"I know. You're not alone in that. It's eatin' up me and Lou, too." He dropped his hand and reached for his beer, taking a long swallow.

"There's got to be a way this all connects. Howie Baker killed himself and died with his secrets. We still don't know if he knew shit about Laurel or the Dirty Death. The feds are involved. Agent Carson Phillips worked with Callie's sister Sadie to bring down Mayor Elliott Goodman and the DOLL Agency. Those human trafficking assholes are still out there. We haven't even dealt with that shit yet."

"No. We haven't. Can't take on the whole world at once, Crow."

I didn't need him to tell me that.

"What about that house in the desert? The one we raided with the Tonopah Royal Bastards? Why the fuck does Undertaker have property out in the desert close to Tonopah when his land is on the border of Nevada and California?"

"All good questions."

"I don't like not having the answers, Raven. It leaves the club vulnerable."

"And our women, including your sister."

"Fuck," I spat, swinging back another shot of whiskey.

"Heard from Carrion?"

"No. I haven't seen him since our conversation." The one where he told me that I had to trust him and listen if I wanted to keep Bella and Gail safe.

"Me either. Makes me anxious."

"Right now, we keep a low profile. Watch over The Roost and our ol' ladies. Undertaker's deadline has passed. If he wants to come for us, he will. We'll be ready."

"You callin' in help from the reapers?"

Our brothers in the Tonopah Royal Bastards were a crucial part of my plan. "Already done. Grim said he's sending the best. They should arrive tonight."

Raven slid from the stool. "Church?"

"Yeah. We got a lot of shit to discuss."

It turned out that I never got away to meet Bella for dinner. I sent her a few texts, and she didn't seem upset, but I hated that I had to cancel.

The hour had grown late by the time I returned to the apartment I shared with Bella on the upper floor of The Roost. I'd spent far too many late nights away from her lately, and guilt swept through me. We'd fucked often, but it wasn't the quality time she'd asked for. I longed to drop everything and hold her close, giving her whatever she wanted. There was nothing I wouldn't do for my queen.

Carrion knew this. It was why he made me promise. My chest ached as I entered, noting almost all the lights were out. Shit. She was already in bed. I didn't see the light from her phone to indicate she was reading. When this was over, I'd do right by her.

As I entered our bedroom, I could tell Bella slept from the rumpled blankets on the bed, and I didn't want to wake her. The moonlight filtering through the window was too dim to make out her features, but I didn't need to see her beauty to know my ol' lady was there.

I slowly stripped off my cut and draped it over a chair. My keys and wallet were placed on my dresser. Kicking off my boots, I sat on the edge of the mattress and reached for her, needing that tiny bit of connection to her to ground me. With Carrion's revelations and the urge to hunt down Undertaker, I had to hold her.

Something wet and sticky coated my fingers as I slid them over the large mounds, not feeling warmth or catching that unmistakable sweet scent of hers that always lingered in my room and on my clothes.

For a split second, terror overtook me. I couldn't move. I struggled to breathe.

My crow croaked outside, his throat rattling as he cried out.

And then I stood, rushed to the lamp, and flipped the switch, illuminating the room and my bed. Red. All I fucking saw was red. It splashed the walls. Streaked across the mattress. Stained everything in my vicinity.

Blood. *So much fucking blood.*

But it wasn't Bella. It wasn't human.

There, in the middle of my bed, was a fucking deer carcass. The throat had been slashed. It bled out on my sheets and comforter where Bella and I slept.

Someone would pay for this.

But where was my Bella? And why was her scent gone? Like she'd been erased? No hint of her perfume or body wash. No lingering sweetness or floral undertones.

I rushed to the bathroom. All her shit was gone. Like someone had packed it all up, and she'd left. Forever. *Just like Laurel.*

Where. The. Fuck. Was. My. Woman.

I nearly panicked, scooping up my cut to thrust my arms through the sleeves, shoving my feet back into my boots, rushing from my room, and thundering down the stairs. Every step threatened to break me apart.

My heart thudded against my ribcage as it beat so hard I thought it would crash through my chest. I entered the bar. . .and *total fucking chaos.*

Sadie, Callie's sister, stood beside a man I didn't know. They were drenched in blood.

Deer blood? What the fuck was happening?

"Where's Bella?" I roared as the room grew quiet.

Everyone turned to stare, noticing the crimson stains on my hands and jeans.

Sadie shook her head. "He took her."

"Who?" I growled.

"Undertaker."

My mouth opened, and agony unleashed. All the pain, fear, and rage I felt from Rook's death, combined with the knowledge that my enemy had taken my mate. My Bella.

She was gone.

A single word rumbled up my chest, bursting free from my lips. "Kraaaaaa!"

The door flew open from outside, and my eyes opened, immediately focusing on whoever entered next. If it was the Dirty Death or Undertaker, I'd shoot without hesitation.

I never would have guessed who stepped through with a timid smile. The years had given her more wrinkles and aged her, but she was still beautiful.

After all this time, she'd finally returned.

My mother.

Laurel Holmes.

And just like Lou predicted, she was alive.

16

Chapter 4

BELLA

Four hours earlier

CROW COULDN'T MAKE OUR date. I knew it was a possibility, but it still stung. It wasn't personal. He just kept getting pulled away because of all the shit with the Dirty Death. Undertaker and his club were monsters. They murdered Crow's father, Rook, weeks before we met. It escalated the rivalry and turned into a vicious war.

But that wasn't why I hated that ruthless son of a bitch. He sent his V.P. Chronos to kidnap my sister. He ordered him to break her. For eight days, he kept her prisoner and violated her, and that nightmare still haunted Bree. She jumped at loud noises and screamed awake at night. She didn't know that I could hear her across the hall. Since Raven was the V.P., his rooms were next to ours.

Today, like so many since her capture, I lingered outside her door. She'd taken a nap, exhausted from early pregnancy.

I slumped outside the door, resting my back against it, and winced. I would have barged in if Raven wasn't there.

He came to check on her and ran inside, rushing into their shared room before I had a chance to say anything. It was probably for the best. Things were still a little stilted with Bree. She hated feeling like a victim. I couldn't seem to stop thinking about her being one.

A sigh escaped as I slowly stood. Sitting here, feeling helpless, wasn't my idea of a good time. I turned, nearly bumping into Lou's scooter.

"Hey, Bella. Wanna ride?" He wiggled his eyebrows.

"Lou," I laughed, catching his double meaning. He was the only one who could have said that to me and gotten away with it. Since the day he hired me, we'd flirted and joked. I loved this old guy. Since dating Crow, I hadn't worked at the bar at Bull's Saloon often. But when the threats with Undertaker increased, I stopped working for Lou altogether.

It made me happy to see him nearly every day since he made a point of visiting me and Bree and sitting in his favorite spot in The Roost's bar.

"I can see it, ya know."

"What?" I asked, refusing to let all the emotion I felt surface.

"That pain you're hidin'. You keep it all bottled up and place that pretty smile on your face. But old Lou knows. I don't like it." He smacked the arm of his chair, rattling the scooter. "That's it. We're gonna go rustle up trouble."

I swallowed the sudden lump in my throat. "You see too much, Lou."

He waved me forward as he turned his ride around. "Let's go."

I followed him to the elevator Rook had installed a couple of years ago when Lou could no longer walk. Crow told me the story the night we met and came here after our date at Hoover Dam. I didn't know it then, but my life was forever altered.

I think I fell in love with Crow almost from the first moment he spoke. He had such a powerful, cocky, but sincere presence.

He was a big man, nearly six foot five. Toned and muscled and thick. Crow had impossibly broad shoulders and short dark hair that he occasionally shaved off. His full lips kissed me more thoroughly than any man ever had, above the waist and below it. He wore a beard, and damn, I loved to run my fingers through it. His presence held me spellbound when he gave me his number, and I still felt that way.

It seemed like fate had destined us to be together.

Lou led me to the kitchen, where he opened the fridge and pulled out a tray. Sliced fruit, various types of cheese, crackers, and dip were arranged in a tempting display. A second tray held an assortment of ham, turkey, and roast beef. "Grab a big plate. We're gettin' a snack."

I wanted to argue that the trays might be saved for something special but fuck it. I wanted some of it, and it looked delicious.

Lou smiled when I filled a plate with the goodies, including cookies and brownies Bree had made that afternoon. She wouldn't care if we ate them. That was why she made them to begin with. "What do you want to drink?"

"Red wine. You?"

"Beer."

We loaded his basket with a few bottles of our preferred beverage, and I held the plate as he led the way outdoors. The sun had already sunk below the horizon, and the stars began to pop into view, dotting the horizon with twinkling lights.

Lou pulled up next to me at the picnic table. "Dig in. I'm starved."

I reached for a hunk of cheddar and made a mini sandwich with a club cracker and a piece of ham. Yum! All this needed was a little Dijon mustard. I'd have to remember that next time. Reaching for the fruit next, I alternated between the meat and cheese and strawberries, cantaloupe, and grapes.

We ate in silence until we'd cleaned the plate. Lou burped and opened his beer, taking a few pulls before he ticked his chin at me.

"You need me, I'm here. That's all I'm gonna say about it."

"I know, and I appreciate that, Lou. I'm just worried about Bree."

"And Crow. The club. Gail. The list is endless, huh?"

I couldn't resist a smile. "Does it get any easier?"

"Not when you're the president or his ol' lady," he admitted truthfully.

"What about when you're scootin' around and pokin' in everyone's business?" I joked.

He snickered. "You got me there."

"I love that you're around, Lou. I mean that."

"I know ya do, honey. You and Bree," he paused and cleared his throat, "You're like family to me. Daughters I never had. I like to ensure you're both being looked after, and no one is messin' with ya."

"Nobody does, Lou. They wouldn't dare. Crow and Raven would lose their shit."

"Yeah," he agreed, "and rightfully so."

"You're special to us too. I can speak for Bree because she's said it to me more than once. We both love you." I leaned over and placed a kiss on his cheek.

He grinned, pushing up the nasal cannula he always wore as it slipped from his nose. Lou never left home without his portable tank. His nurse insisted on it. Lou kept an extra in his basket at the front of the scooter. "Now that'll give me some good dreams."

I giggled, pouring wine into my glass and swirling the contents before taking a sip. "This is nice. For once, I feel relaxed."

"That's because you're almost halfway through that bottle of wine."

He wasn't wrong.

I opened my mouth to reply when I saw something sail through the air and sink into his thigh. A little red object. It looked like a dart.

Lou frowned. "The hell?"

A second one lodged into his left arm as he cursed.

"Run, Bella!" His voice slurred.

Shit! There were drugs in those darts!

I slipped from the table and crouched, trying to move around the edge so I could clear a path to the door. My gaze swept over the lot, noting the bodies that slumped over or already lay on the ground. How the hell did we miss this?

I knew I should have screamed. It would have brought people running from The Roost. But I realized it would also place the people I loved in even greater danger. Bree didn't need to be traumatized again. Raven would protect her.

Crow was busy in church with most of the club members. They wouldn't notice what was happening until it was too late.

Lou staggered from his scooter when the first Dirty Death MC member reached us. His fist swung at the attacker, but he missed. Whatever drug the DDMC used, it was potent.

I cried out when the asshole punched Lou, knocking him against the picnic table. "Hey! Leave him alone!"

Lou's voice sounded panicked as he begged me to get to safety. He knew my choice as I refused to say a word, flinching when I stood, and a dart hit my leg. My vision blurred as I swayed.

Another DDMC member moved from the shadows and lifted a pistol, whipping it against the back of Lou's skull. Lou collapsed against the table, draping over the top and landing on his stomach. I wish they hadn't done that. There wasn't a reason to hurt the old guy. He was harmless.

21

A dark figure moved in front of me. A black faceless mask hid his features. "Undertaker is expecting you, Bella Hart." He lifted a syringe and plunged it into my neck.

I felt a pinch. A burst of pain at the injection. Then nothing.

Only darkness as I felt my body go limp.

MY EYES FLUTTERED AS I slowly awakened. I noted that I felt cold, which was odd considering it was summer. The chill didn't feel like air conditioning. It was more like a damp, moldy cold that penetrated my skin and left me shivering.

It was dark. I couldn't see much. Something scurried close by and bumped into my ankle. I jolted, pushed off the ground, and crashed into a wall. A stone exterior. My fingertips pressed against the smooth surface, dipping into the grooves.

I kicked as I felt another furry body skitter over my foot. "Ah!"

Dark laughter echoed from across the room. The sound bounced off the walls. "Humans. Natural selection should have bred you from existence. You have no desirable traits, no way to protect yourself from the beasts and monsters."

Oh, God. That deep, sinister voice. It was terrifying.

"Such a pity your eyesight is so poor."

I heard a shuffle as he moved, coming closer. My back flattened against the wall. "What do you want?"

"Isn't it obvious? Come now. You're one of the smarter ones."

"Crow," I whispered.

"Bingo," he growled.

"You're Undertaker." I didn't have to ask.

"Yes."

"You owe me," I blurted, pushing off the wall and moving toward the sound of his voice. "I demand restitution."

"You demand?" Laughter, albeit tinged with irritation, followed.

"Yes. It's my right."

A lightbulb flickered on, and I stood a few feet from iron bars, alone in a jail cell on a muddy floor. A beast of a man was across from me, staring through the bars.

I blinked, adjusting to the light as he reached out and gripped the iron barrier. Something about him was off. Not in the deranged, psychopath way, even if I could tell that was true. No, this was different.

"You sense it. Interesting."

I shrugged. "I want retribution for my sister. I demand it," I repeated.

His lips twitched as if he wanted to smile. "You don't fear me."

"What point would that make? I know you're bigger and stronger and could kill me if you wanted. I'd be dead by now if that were your goal. So, no, I'm not afraid. I'm fucking pissed."

He tilted back his head and howled with laughter, like an actual howl. It reminded me of a wolf. "You're a good match for the crow. I see now why he mated you."

That wasn't important. "Bree was assaulted. Chronos raped her. He beat her." My voice cracked. "I want justice!"

"He's dead. There's no further blood to be spilled."

"That's not good enough." I approached the bars, slamming my palm against them. "Crow got vindication. Not me. It's not the same."

"No," he agreed, "it's not."

"Then you understand."

"I do."

Good.

"But I can't grant it. Not yet."

"Why?"

"Because you're bait."

Oh. Fuck.

Chapter 5

UNDERTAKER

Present time

"ON YOUR KNEES," I growled, shoving on the slim shoulder of the nameless young woman in front of me. She was the third one I'd pulled into my room in the last hour. Frustration pulsed through my veins. The vargulf was agitated. He wanted to fuck. I wanted my mate.

My cock had hardened with the need for sex, but I couldn't seem to complete the act. Me. The goddamn Alpha. Every time I tried to shove my erection into a warm, waiting hole, I pictured Sadie's face. It felt like a betrayal.

Why the fuck was this happening!?

I'd fucked other women since we met. Hell, I shared a bed and fucked more than one while she masturbated next to me. We both got off at the same time. I'd cuddled with her afterward.

She should be here. Now. *With me.*

Taking my cock and loving it.

My head lifted, and I sniffed. Sadie's scent was beginning to fade. That only made it worse.

"Open your mouth. Wider."

I shoved the long length of my erection inside, grasping the blonde hair in front of me as my hips surged forward, ramming the back of her throat in the process. I had to shut my eyes, pretending it was Sadie on her knees. Dark hair. A sweet smile. Eyes that shimmered with lust and need.

My hips swayed, driving deep, even when I heard the girl choking. She sputtered around my girth, but I didn't relent. I couldn't. The vargulf grew excited. He pumped down the willing throat and enjoyed the saliva that dripped from the quivering mouth. He saw only a means to satisfy himself.

For the first time, I felt disgust. The conflict waged a war inside me. I wanted to stop him. This wasn't how the Alpha acted. I didn't have to force a woman into my bed. They came willingly. *But that was before the vargulf took over.*

A sneer dominated my lips, and my fangs elongated, a partial shift allowing my claws to break through my fingernails. I could slice this female's delicate neck with a flick of my wrist. The pain of that semi transformation sharpened my focus.

And that was the moment I realized I was no longer fully controlled by the vargulf. He didn't dictate my every thought and action. His thoughts and mine. . . *separated.* Two beings. One body. A shared soul.

It never occurred to me until now that becoming the vargulf had ripped away my human/wolf side. I'd assumed it was consumed with the merger. But now I understood it was a deception created by the vargulf. A means to keep me submissive to his demands, to follow out his carnal appetites, and to kill without mercy.

Wolves were not bloodthirsty, mindless killers. That was the vargulf—his requirement for the privilege of combining our essence and becoming one with the monster.

Until now, I hadn't realized how much I'd given up. He almost destroyed my wolf and the man I had once been. The thoughts raced through my mind as I felt the vargulf's excitement. He liked that the girl reached out and gripped his legs. She tilted her head back, allowing deeper penetration.

Shocked, I realized he didn't know what I felt.

We had somehow. . . unlinked.

My body went through the motions, shuddering as I spilled my seed, growling when the girl swallowed it down. I felt nothing. The enjoyment belonged entirely to the vargulf.

It was strange. He didn't seem to notice the alteration.

I could feel everything he wanted, desired, and needed. It no longer dominated my every thought or overtook my will but dug in with sharp, painful barbs. I winced, but no change in facial expressions betrayed the pathway of my thoughts or the confusion that slowly gave way to rage.

He tricked me, used me, and bent my will like every other being he deceived since our merger. Everything was always about fulfilling his needs and objectives.

Even the war with the Devil's Murder MC.

And that was when the conflict became too much. The fury over my son Fang's death gave way to sorrow and the truth that he was also to blame for the accident that night. He was so stubborn, so defiant. Fang had to learn everything the hard way. He bucked against my will as Alpha.

But. . . did he? Was that only the perception of the vargulf?

Noooooooooo.

My son. Dead. Why did he rush off that night? What happened? I had no memory of those final moments before he sped off on his motorcycle. I struggled with blame and agony over his loss.

My head began to pound with a sudden ache, like a dozen hammers were battering against my skull at once. My vision blurred. The vargulf stilled as he sensed something was off.

"Get out," he roared to the girl who scrambled to listen.

The door slammed shut as she left us alone.

Fatigue pressed in, and I stumbled to my bed. I flopped onto the mattress as my vision darkened. Before I lost consciousness, I made a vow to discover the truth, and if the vargulf killed my son, I would destroy him.

THE VARGULF REGAINED CONTROL.

When I awakened, his mind almost completely shut out my thoughts. I felt his triumph when he knew I figured it out.

So, he wanted to battle wills. Fine.

The vargulf forgot one crucial detail. He was a beast, but I was the Alpha. I had access to power he would never be able to use without my consent, and I didn't fucking give it. Not anymore. Now, I was fighting two wars. One with the vargulf. The second with those fucking crows.

Game on, motherfuckers.

The vargulf still couldn't hear what I thought. Sure, he bulldozed back into control, but now that I wasn't unconscious, he couldn't maintain it. The Alpha wolf part of me wouldn't allow it.

He snarled as I stood, marching toward the bathroom to shower. I stripped, tossing my clothes onto the floor. My shoulders rolled back as I cracked my neck, noting the stiffness in the joints. Turning the water as hot as I could stand, I let the steam build up and stepped under the spray. The heat penetrated the muscles, and I began to relax, grabbing shampoo to lather into my hair.

Once I finished, I soaped up my body, pausing to stroke my growing erection.

Fuck. My thoughts drifted to my female. My beautiful mate.

Sadie. I didn't dare say her name out loud. I didn't want the vargulf to focus on my woman. He didn't deserve her.

Christ. I didn't either, but at least I truly desired and needed her, not just to further any agenda.

My hand tightened around my shaft, gliding from root to tip. A groan left my lips as I slapped my free hand on the slippery tile in front of me. I hunched over, gaining speed as my hand moved faster.

All I could think about was Sadie. Our joining. The slick, tight pussy that I dreamed about whenever I shut my eyes. How perfect she'd felt, how warm and wet and inviting. She clenched around me when she came, and I hated that I'd been unable to look into her eyes.

The vargulf had been blinded by Carson Phillips. Her other mate. And he fucking knew how to weaken the vargulf before I did. Smart. Maybe I should consider making him an ally if I didn't end up killing him first.

Sadie had cried out a name when she spasmed around my cock. It wasn't my real name. She never learned it because the vargulf wouldn't allow it. He knew there was power in an Alpha's name.

Fuck. That was how he subdued me.

I pushed the thought aside, focusing on my female again. Sadie. *I need you. Come back to me.*

I felt the magic leave my body with the words, pulsed outward into the atmosphere by my Alpha blood. She would hear it and obey. Not because she didn't have a choice like the vargulf forced her on so many occasions. She would come back to me because she mated my Alpha wolf. The bond demanded it.

But there was more there—a hint of feelings that ran deeper.

I didn't have time to explore this line of thought, not with the vargulf watching my actions. My body needed release.

I pumped faster, snapping my hips back and forth to increase the friction. My thoughts became consumed with my mate. I only wanted to please her, to fill her, and to make her mine again and again until she couldn't deny that she belonged with the Alpha.

A shudder seized my body before I came, coating the wall in the cum I wanted to fill her with instead. The need and drive to procreate almost consumed me. That was another marked difference between the vargulf and me. He didn't need an heir. I did. That desire rose from my wishes alone.

I dragged a ragged breath through my lungs. I had to find a way to separate from the vargulf before he broke my bond with Sadie or killed her to prove a point. He would do it if he thought it would keep me in line.

The vargulf needed to hunt. I'd kept him caged inside me for weeks, increasing his hunger and need for carnage until the feeling made my skin crawl. I did that intentionally, but at the time I decided, I hadn't yet realized why. Now I understood the reason. He was weaker when he fed less often.

He tasted blood for the last time when I marked our mate during the claiming. Sadie's cunt had gripped my cock as I fucked her, but when I bit her and the bond completed, I felt my magic and cum enter her body. She could already be pregnant with my pup. I had to protect her from the vargulf.

Sadie had been gone for weeks now. Long enough for the life inside her to begin to grow and show her signs of her new condition. When I called to her in the shower, I almost felt it. My mate would return to me. Soon.

I needed to prepare for her arrival, but how did I accomplish that without alerting the vargulf?

Over three hundred years ago, my ancestor and alpha to the pack settled this stretch of land on the border of Nevada and California.

We needed woods and a safe place for the Alpha and his pack. Our pups had been born here for generations. My new offspring would be born here, too.

I dressed and left the bathroom. When I reached the lower levels of my ancestral home, wolves had gathered to greet me. They lowered their heads, exposing their necks to show respect to their Alpha.

"What is it?"

"We have the crow female."

"Which one?"

"The president's woman. Bella Hart."

Ah. Good. The faster we moved this war along, the easier it would be to secure my bond with my mate. Of course, I planned to use the crows to accomplish this task. I would need their help to destroy the vargulf.

When Crow and the Devil's Murder refused to send a reply after I released Talon, I had no choice but to act. I sent my swiftest wolves to take Bella. Crow would come for her. No mated male would ever let his female go without a fight.

I never would.

The vargulf was too obsessed with his hatred and need for consumption. He destroyed everything in his path. I didn't see that until the last twenty-four hours. The fault for those who had been wronged belonged with me. I could no longer allow the vargulf's atrocities to continue.

Sadie would return to me and bring Carson. His abilities would help me secure victory. I'd make him agree if I had to do it. I refused to lose my mate.

Bella's arrival ushered the next phase of my plan into place.

"Where is she?"

"In the dungeon as you requested, my Alpha."

"Good. Dismissed."

My pack dispersed as I grinned—time to visit Bella.

In the old, musty cell my pack members placed her in, she rested on a dry patch of ground. Rats scurried by her body, and I growled, chasing most of them away. I had no intention for them to harm her. It defeated my purpose.

Her gaze swept around her when she woke, frantic as the night disguised my presence. I didn't expect her to shove any fear aside and boldly demand justice for her sister. She intrigued me. The vargulf considered her an excellent candidate for his personal pleasure.

I wouldn't allow that either.

Crow would be on his way soon, pissed because I had taken his woman. Good. We needed to settle our differences and the bullshit that led to our rivalry had to be buried if we wanted to survive.

For the first time since merging with the vargulf, I wanted peace.

Chapter 6

CROW

THE BAR SILENCED. NOT a soul spoke as I stared at Laurel. I couldn't think beyond the constricting pain in my chest.

Bella. *Baby. Please be okay.*

I struggled to breathe and clenched my fists, turning from Laurel to meet Raven's shocked expression.

"Fuck," he grunted.

That summed it up.

Hawk rushed inside behind Laurel and nearly slammed into her, knocking her aside. "Shit. Sorry. Pres! It's Lou. He's hurt!"

That finally forced me into action. I rushed outdoors and glanced at my guys on the ground. Why the fuck were they all passed out? What the hell happened?

Lou groaned from the picnic tables, struggling to sit up. He pulled a small object from his thigh with a curse. "Fucking darts, Crow."

Darts? I didn't understand what he meant until I took a seat beside him, staring at the item he placed in my palm. A tranquilizer dart.

"Fuck. They drugged you."

"No, just me. Bella. Everyone outside. They were quick. We never saw or heard anything."

Fucking Undertaker. He planned this shit. Our crows should have heard them approach and sounded the alarm. Why didn't I see any of them in the sky? No caws. Not a single kraa.

Raven noticed at the same time. "There aren't any crows."

I closed my eyes, searching for the connection. I could feel them. They were close. . . but blocked somehow. Strange.

"I can feel my crow," Talon announced, "but something is wrong."

Yeah, that was obvious.

"We'll discuss this in church later." I began giving orders, taking care of those who'd been hit with the darts first. Lou was the only person wounded. The assholes targeted the old man on the scooter. They would answer for that.

"You okay, Lou?"

"My jaw and head are poundin'. Took a right hook and a pistol to the back of my head. I guess they didn't like it when I tried to fight."

Raven chuckled. "You badass motherfucker, Lou."

"Shit," he cursed. "I would've had 'em all beat if Bella wasn't here. I was scared they were gonna hurt her too."

"Did they?" I asked, my voice strained.

"Just a couple of darts." Lou cleared his throat and dropped his voice. "She didn't fight them, Crow."

What? Why?

"I think she believed she was protecting you and everyone else by sacrificing herself. Damn noble but foolish too."

34

"They take anyone else besides her?"

"Not that I saw." He cursed again and rubbed the back of his head. A shrug followed.

"Where's Falcon?" I hollered.

"Here, pres." He joined us, ticking his chin at Lou. "I got you, old timer."

Lou flipped him off.

Yeah, he was fine.

I left Lou as Falon healed his injuries and talked to each member who had been a target of the darts. None could tell me much. It happened fast. Everything had been quiet until they were struck and went down.

There wasn't shit to learn from this other than Undertaker wanted me to go after my woman. He was forcing a confrontation. To be honest, I never understood why it took so long. This shit should have been sorted when Rook was still president.

It didn't matter now. I had to free Bella, and I didn't have time to waste. I'd already lost valuable minutes handling shit here when I really wanted to rush after her and tell everyone else to fuck off and figure it out without me. But that wasn't an option. I was the president of the club, and I had to do my duty.

I rubbed my tired eyes and headed back inside The Roost. The sight that greeted me sent uneasy vibes down my back: two bloody people, Sadie and Carson, sitting at a table with Callie and Hawk. Across from them, Laurel sat alone.

Well, shit. I didn't want to deal with either group. I almost left Raven in charge so I could head out, but I decided against it. This gave me the excuse to be abrupt and to the point.

"Laurel," I greeted her as I stopped in front of her table.

Talon, Raven, and my sister approached. Gail's hand curled around my arm. Fuck. I needed her support right now. That panicky feeling in my chest relaxed just a bit.

"I'm here, Austin."

I squeezed her hand in response.

"Austin," Laurel began.

"That's Crow to you," I corrected.

She sighed. "Crow. I know this is a shock."

"It doesn't matter what this is. I don't have time for it. Bella's been taken."

Laurel rushed to her feet. "By Undertaker?"

What the fuck did she know about it? "Yes."

"That's the reason I'm here. To put things right and clear up the past."

"There isn't shit to put right. You fucking left when I was seven years old. Walked out of my life and stayed gone."

"Crow," she whispered, flinching with my words.

"Don't give me that innocent act. Do you know what that did to me? How many nights I cried for my fucking mother? Have any idea how hard and confusing that was?"

"I can explain."

"I don't care about your fucking explanation."

I'd reached the end of my patience.

"I have a letter from Rook. He-he told me to show it to you if something happened to him. He said it would help."

Help what? The loss and trauma of my youth?

"I don't want to read it," I snarled.

"Austin," Gail whispered. "Take it. You don't have to read it now."

Laurel held out the letter, and I snatched it from her hand.

"Leave. I can't deal with this right now."

Laurel nodded. "I know. For what it's worth, I'm sorry, Austin."

Too fucking late for that now. The damage was already done.

"I'm staying at a hotel. Come find me when you're ready. Room 315 at Sunset Station."

I didn't reply. My hand almost crumpled the letter as she walked out of The Roost. My heart ached for a new reason, and I had to brush the feeling aside.

"I'll go with you whenever you want."

I tugged my sister into a hug. This was too much. All at once. I was this fucking close to losing my shit. "Gail," I managed to croak.

"It's okay, Austin. It's gonna be okay."

I released her to walk to Sadie. "We need to talk, but I can't delay any longer." I gulped in air, trying to calm the fuck down. Bella needed me. "Did you bring that fucking deer into my bedroom?"

"You're right. We can't delay."

"Answer me!" I roared, and everyone in the vicinity shut up.

"Yes. I had to do it. Carson and I are coming with you. I'll explain on the way."

"It's not safe, Sadie." Callie reached for her sister. "Stay here. Don't go back to Undertaker."

"I know you don't understand, sis, but I've got to do this."

Callie dropped her hands. "I don't. He's hurt you."

"I've hurt him too. Not the vargulf." She sighed. "It won't make sense now, but it will later."

"Pres." I turned my head, watching as Carrion appeared, walking toward me as he materialized from the shadows. "You're gonna save Bella."

I gripped the letter in my hand and almost fucking cried with relief. "You're sure?"

"Now? Yes. It had to be this way."

I trusted him. "I'm leaving. Now." I stuffed the letter into a pocket inside my cut. I'd read it later because it wasn't as important as Bella.

Whatever words haunted me from the past weren't helping my present.

"Raven, I need you here. If anything happens, you'll the lead the club."

He dipped his chin. "You got it, pres."

"Hawk, Cuckoo, and Claw, you're with me. Carrion?"

"I'll be riding out now."

Noted. He left as I turned back to Raven. "I don't suspect anything will go down while I'm not here, but stay sharp. Rael, Exorcist, and Patriot should arrive soon from Tonopah."

"I got this, pres. Go."

SINCE I NEEDED TO talk to Sadie and I wasn't sure if Bella would be able to ride when I found her, I opted to take one of the company vehicles. Hawk, Cuckoo, and Claw rode behind us. I assumed Carrion scouted the way ahead of our location down Hwy 95.

"Lake Alpine is how far?" I asked, turning around to ask Sadie. She sat behind Carson, who volunteered to drive.

"About eight hours."

Eight fucking hours. A lot could happen in that amount of time. None of it good.

"Why did you put that fucking deer in my bed?" I asked, folding my arms across my chest. "No bullshit."

"I needed to do it."

"Clarify what that means."

"Undertaker threatened me and my sister. I had to follow through, or it would have gotten back to him."

Not a great explanation, but it sufficed. "How did you meet Undertaker?"

"On a case over three years ago."

"I placed her undercover to help catch the men who were trafficking girls in the Las Vegas area," Carson added.

"We built a case against some of the traffickers, Mayor Elliott Goodman, and the Dirty Death MC. I had to get close to him. He liked me." Sadie shrugged.

Damn. That was dangerous.

"Why did you do it?"

"I didn't give her a choice," Carson answered.

Sadie smirked. "He didn't expect to fall for me."

"Yeah," Carson agreed. "That's true."

She turned her attention back to me. "Undertaker is unpredictable. You know this. But what you don't know is that he's not just a vargulf."

"Fuck." Of course, it wasn't that easy. "What is he?"

"He's an Alpha wolf. The leader of his clan."

Yeah. So?

"It means he's fighting an internal war. I've seen it."

Carson gripped the steering wheel and shot a glance at her in the rearview mirror.

What the fuck did that mean?

"Explain."

"I told him he had to cut ties with his vargulf to be with me. I never expected him to do it."

Well, shit. "He bit you?"

"Yes. He mated me, Crow. The Alpha. I, uh, I'm pregnant too."

Jesus. Christ. She slept with that fucking bastard?

"The thing is, I care about his wolf. The Alpha. That part of him is good. It's the vargulf that's evil. Everything awful he's done has been the vargulf. I know his human/wolf side didn't want it."

How could she possibly know that?

"You could be wrong."

"He told me when he slept. The vargulf would rest, and the Alpha would wake, eager to protect and be with me. We bonded on those long, lonely nights."

Carson grumbled, but I wasn't listening to what he was saying.

"But I know how to free him, Crow."

Now, that got my attention. "You know how to defeat the vargulf?"

"Partially, yes. I need to use the Alpha's real name."

"I'm guessing he told you when the vargulf was sleeping."

"He did."

"What if he's tricking you?"

"I thought of that. But then he did something I didn't expect."

"Yeah?"

"He asked me to kill him."

The fuck?

"He's afraid the vargulf will harm me. All the Alpha wants is his mate and child. He's willing to do whatever it takes to protect me. That's our ace. It's the reason we can defeat the vargulf."

Interesting assumption. "So what does this all have to do with him?" I ticked my chin at Carson.

Sadie smiled. "He's my mate too."

Christ. I wish I didn't ask.

I glanced at Carson. "What the fuck are you?"

He smirked. "I'm a warlock."

Werewolves. Vargulf. Crows. And now a goddamn warlock. "How many fucking supernatural beings are there?" I asked sarcastically.

Carson snorted. "Is that a serious question?"

"Look, man. I ride a motorcycle and lead my club. We have our bond with the crows. I don't need more."

"I get that. The more your eyes open, the more your world grows. Your need to protect your woman and your club is your life. Adding more only complicates things. It's a lot."

True.

"I can channel magic from the earth and use the elements. It's tricky and exhausting, but with the right combination, I can bend it to my will."

"Okay." I didn't want to know how that was possible.

Sadie leaned forward, bracing her elbows on her knees. "The vargulf believes my bond with Carson was broken when he mated me. But what he doesn't know is that the vargulf can't mate. He can fuck and cum, but he can't procreate. It's why he needs to possess an Alpha. Their virility ensures breeding can continue."

"So his Alpha wolf got you pregnant. He wants to die to save you and defeat the vargulf, and the two of you are gonna use magic and say the Alpha's name to break the vargulf's hold over him."

"Yes." Sadie beamed a smile. "See? It's not that complicated."

The fuck it wasn't. I didn't say shit.

If this plan helped me rescue Bella, I would go along with it.

Chapter 7

ℬELLA

UNDERTAKER LEFT ME IN that cell for hours. I didn't have my phone, and it aggravated me that I had to keep kicking away rats in this hellhole. I was dirty, thirsty, tired, and worried about Crow. When he figured out that I was missing, he would lose his shit. Worse, he might do something stupid to get me back. I could handle that if I wasn't so sure Undertaker might try to kill him.

"Hey," I yelled for what had to be the twentieth time. "You can't keep me in here forever!"

"Actually," a soft voice contradicted, "I think he can."

Surprised, I blinked, rushing to the bars to stare as best I could through the gaps. To the left, down one cell, a young woman with blonde hair styled in braids waved. She looked as dirty and exhausted as I felt. "Hi. How long have you been here?"

"I'm not sure. Weeks?"

Shit. "Did Undertaker kidnap you?"

She shook her head, backing away from the bars.

43

"Hey! Sorry! We don't have to talk about that."

She moved close again, resting her forehead against the cool metal. "I'm Rebecca, but I like to be called Rebel."

Cute. "My name is Bella. Nice to meet you, Rebel."

"Is it? Really?"

"Meeting you? Yes. Being here? Hell no."

The corners of her lips twitched like she fought a smile. It was hard to tell in the dim light.

"Do they ever give us water?" I asked as my mouth felt dry.

"Twice a day. Sunrise and sunset. That's when they give us food, too."

I didn't ask what they provided.

"You'll get out of here."

"Why do you say that?" I wondered.

"Because you stood up to him. He liked it."

She heard that conversation with Undertaker.

"He hurt my sister."

"He's hurt a lot of people."

Yeah, I bet. That was probably why she was here, too. Maybe he killed someone she loved.

I opened my mouth to reply when I heard the sound of metal creaking and a key turning the lock at the top of the stairs. I could see far enough down the length of the cells to make out the bottom of them. Concrete. We were at least fifteen feet below ground level.

Heavy boots thundered down the stairs as the beast heaved his bulk in my direction. "You're being set free," he announced as he stopped in front of my cell.

"Why? Am I getting my retribution now?"

He snorted. "Something like that."

What the hell did that mean?

Undertaker shoved a key into the lock, pausing as he stared at me. He seemed to be considering something. "When I open this gate, you should run."

I didn't want to ask. Nothing good would come from his answer. I felt it deep in my bones. This wasn't freedom. It was a test. Or maybe, an opportunity. "Should I be asking questions? Do they matter?"

"No," he growled, "but I will tell you that your vindication is out in my forest if you can survive long enough to obtain it."

So, yes, a test. I had to survive whatever awaited me. "Can I have a lighter?"

He tilted his head to the side, thinking it over. "Just this one item. That's it." His fingers plucked a metal lighter from his pocket. "Here."

I took it from him, shoved it deep into the front pocket of my jean shorts, and cracked my neck. Jumping up and down, I prepared my body to run. I had grown cold and stiff in that cell, but now adrenaline began to pulse through my veins. "I'm ready."

"Bella Hart?"

"Yeah?"

"You might be the first to make it."

The first? Shit!

He opened the gate, and I rushed past him, running for the stairs, climbing them quickly, and shooting out of the underground cells at nearly top speed. The sudden light almost blinded me, but I forced myself to focus on the line of trees ahead.

And that was when I heard it. Multiple howls. A chorus that rose in pitch and lengthened in duration as if they bayed at the rising sun instead of a moon. Overlapping one another, they heralded my doom.

It didn't matter. Only survival and getting my retribution for Bree. I pumped my arms and legs, desperate to reach the edge of the forest. It loomed ahead as mist began to roll along the tall grass.

Undertaker told the truth. I was bait. The hunt had begun, and he invited his entire pack to participate.

I made it to the trees and didn't stop, knowing I had to keep moving. When I slowed down, they would find me. There was no guarantee they weren't close now, but I had to try to outrun the wolves.

If I hadn't known what Undertaker and his club were, this would have been a shock. Crow prepared me for this when he described his bond to his crow. Wolves shared a bond with their human side, too. Crow had shared about his enemy to ensure I understood the threat against the club.

My lungs began to burn as I heaved air into them. I couldn't keep this up. I wasn't in terrible shape, but I didn't run marathons either. A painful twitch in my right side slowly got worse as I slowed, pausing for a few seconds to listen. Somewhere, I heard water trickling over rocks.

There had to be a river or a lake close.

If I wanted to survive, I had to mask my scent. I probably smelled like that jail cell, and my clothes stunk. The wolves would pick up on that odor.

It didn't take long to find the stream that spilled into a lake. I could tell from where I stood on the bank that it was deep in the middle. I'd always been a good swimmer. I decided to take my chances with the water over the wolves.

It was fucking cold as I stepped into it, going slow in order not to splash and cause too many ripples on the surface. The sun would rise high soon, around the time I'd reach the other side. A swim that should wash most of the stench from my clothes. It would be hot, and I'd dry off quickly.

This had to work.

When I finally waded out far enough to submerge my shoulders, I ducked under the surface and began to swim underwater. The temperature didn't bother me with the consistent movement, but my shoes felt heavy, forcing me to travel slower.

I surfaced before I wanted.

My gaze bounced around the lake, but I didn't see anyone. No wolves. No animals. Just a clear blue sky, trees, and a bright summer sun. This would have been nice if I wasn't on the run.

It took five more trips to the surface to reach the other side of the lake. After waiting in the water for long minutes, hovering behind a grouping of large rocks, I finally left it.

I swam toward the shore when I noticed a pathway to the right, hidden mainly by overhanging rocks. It was in the path of the sun, but from both shorelines, I would be hidden from view if I hugged the inside wall of tree roots, rock, and packed dirt.

I waded toward that area, hoping my luck prevailed. My shoes were soaked and squished as I walked, but I was clear of the lake. The heat of the day had risen, and I felt my clothes begin to dry. Something might go my way after all.

I thought about the lighter I'd gotten from Undertaker and realized it was useless now after my lengthy swim. I ruined it. Shit.

My body felt more worn out than I wanted to admit. It wasn't the most pleasant walk. I chafed a little from the denim shorts, and my feet hurt. I developed a slight headache.

But I was alive. I'd made it this far.

And then a howl rose from the trees ahead.

CROW

"DO YOU KNOW WHY the war with the Dirty Death and my club started?" I asked, glancing between Carson and Sadie.

"Fang's death," Carson answered. "Undertaker's son. From what I understand, it was an accident."

"It was," I confirmed, "but shit escalated when Undertaker's property taxes weren't paid. He lost his land because my father paid them. Rook owns the deed to a hundred acres of ancestral land that the wolves consider sacred ground."

Carson whistled. "Damn. No wonder he's so pissed. Rook was a genius. He could sell it back to him or use it to obtain a truce."

"I'm not sure. He never told me about it. I didn't know it existed until Gail found the deed in our basement."

Thinking of my father led me back to Laurel's visit and the note she'd given me. I reached inside my cut and retrieved it, finally feeling like it was the right time to read it.

Austin,

> *Son, forgive me for all the deception. I had to follow through with everything down to the smallest detail, or Carrion said you wouldn't survive.*

Oh, shit. Carrion? But when would he have told my father? He wasn't around when I was a kid. Hell, he wasn't much older than me. It wasn't possible.

But then I remembered my conversation with Carrion only a couple of days earlier.

"You'll need to trust me, pres. When the time is right, stay out of it."

"You're asking me not to step in and protect my woman?"

"Her life depends on it."

Fuck! "Carrion. You can't ask that of me."

"I have to," he replied sadly. "If you don't listen to me, she won't make it."

Nooooooo.

"This is war. We're going to lose people. It can't be helped. But it's the specific people we'll lose that can be altered."

"Fuck."

"And that's a very tiny window open to keep Gail and Bella alive."

"Are you telling me I could lose my ol' lady and my sister?"

"Yes."

I shuddered. Fear slithered down my spine.

"Do what I say when I say so. No hesitation. No argument. Just do it. The clock has already begun to count down."

Rook must have had a similar experience. I didn't know how Carrion contacted him, but he did it. There was no other explanation for why my mother would have this letter, written in my father's handwriting, dated eighteen years earlier.

My gaze flicked back to the letter.

There are things I've done, decisions I had to make to keep you and your sister alive. Gail is special.

You need to keep her away from the vargulf. Undertaker's evil side will covet her. He'll want to possess her gifts, and he'll end up killing her.

Right now, we hold a bargaining chip. The deed to his land. Carrion told me the right time to purchase it. It's all we've got to prevent the vargulf from slaughtering us all.

He needs that land. It belonged to his ancestors. Every generation of his pack has been born on those lands. His new offspring need to be born there, too. It'll drive the rotten magic out and banish the vargulf. Undertaker's child is a true Alpha male. He'll lead his pack and bring peace.

This is a lot. I know it'll sound unbelievable. Carrion seemed to believe you would accept it after Bella was taken. He said it had to be this way.

By the time you read this, your relationship with your mother will be shit. Give Laurel a chance. For me.

She'll tell you the truth if you're brave enough to hear it.

I love you, son.

Your dad, Rook

Fuck.

What the hell did Carrion see that prompted all of this?

"Pull over, Carson."

"Why?"

"I gotta piss."

"Shit. I do, too."

He eased the SUV off the road and onto the median, slowing to a stop. I opened the car door and walked a short distance away to a crop of trees.

Once I finished draining my bladder, I called Carrion.

He answered before it rang. Creepy. "Yeah, pres?"

"I read Rook's letter."

"Then you know it had to all go down just like this."

I guess. Part of me didn't want to accept it. "What you said about Gail. Is she safe?"

He paused, and I knew if I was with him, I'd see his eyes roll back in his head, and only the white portion would be visible.

"For now."

"Can that change?"

"Shit can always change, Crow. That's why I stay connected."

Connected? "What do you mean?"

"The spirit world. The crows guide me."

Wow. "Where are they?"

"Waiting."

Was that why we didn't see them at The Roost? Were they told not to be around when Undertaker sent his pack to fetch Bella?

"Will they be there when I need them?"

He scoffed. "Always. They're part of us. You know that."

"If this is a success, I'll keep Bella and Gail alive, right? They'll be okay?"

"Yeah."

"Who," I paused and cleared my throat, "Who will we lose?"

"Even I can't predict that, pres."

I didn't like that answer, but I could live with it. "Don't go dark on me."

"I won't."

We ended the call, and I walked back to the SUV. Carson and Sadie were waiting.

"We're good. Let's go." I climbed inside and shut the door. "Only about an hour left before we reach pack lands."

Chapter 8

CROW

CARSON SPED UP AS we approached the main gate outside Undertaker's compound. His foot pressed the accelerator to the floorboard. "Hang on!"

"Shit!" I yelled, bracing for impact as he bulldozed through with the SUV and crashed the barrier, dragging the gate with us for several feet before it flew off and clattered a short distance away.

Behind us, I heard the rumble of engines and glanced in the rearview to see that Hawk, Claw, and Cuckoo had followed. I didn't know if Carrion had arrived or not. I didn't see him or his bike, but that didn't mean shit. He never used conventional travel methods. I wouldn't be surprised if he was hiding in the forest somewhere, already using the shadows to track Bella.

We finally made it after eight fucking hours on the road. I was antsy as fuck to find my woman and finally get justice for Rook. With any luck, it would happen today.

Carson pulled to a stop outside a huge house. Mansion, to be precise. Undertaker was living well on this land.

Too bad he didn't fucking own it any longer.

I flung the door open and jumped out, palming my gun as I approached the house. My club brothers were right behind me. There wasn't a need to kick down the door since it was unlocked when I checked the knob. The front door swung open, and we entered, spreading out to cover our asses in case of trouble.

No one was there. Not a fucking soul greeted us.

Frowning, I continued to move from room to room, searching for Undertaker or any of his pack members. After a thorough search, we came up empty.

Down a long hall, we entered the bar. Oddly enough, it resembled ours. Lots of stools, leather couches, pool tables, neon liquor signs, and a wall of glass behind the rows of liquor. The Dirty Death logo hung on one wall, and another was filled with framed photos of club members.

I itched to burn the fucking place to the ground, but I didn't have time to deal with this shit.

The entire fucking house was deserted. And now I was pissed.

Where was Bella?

We exited the bar, meeting Carson and Sadie by the SUV. Something was up. It had to be a trap. I didn't put it past Undertaker to try to lure me into his forest where his pack had the advantage and could ambush us. They were fucking wolves.

A lone howl lifted into the air.

My gaze swung toward the trees. "They're not here. No one is." Realization hit me in the chest, and I almost stumbled as I took a step forward. "They're hunting."

"Oh, no," Sadie gasped.

"The pack is hunting Bella," Carson guessed. "You need to go!"

Fuck!

"You find Undertaker. Do your part. I'm going after my ol' lady." I didn't stick around for a reply, racing toward the trees as I heard Hawk, Claw, and Cuckoo follow.

It was eerily quiet when we entered. Not even birds flew overhead or chirped within this forest. We still hadn't seen or heard from the crows. I didn't have time to worry about that right now. Bella was my only concern. Once I had her, I'd get her to safety and take care of Undertaker. He wasn't escaping my revenge.

The club wanted vengeance for Rook, and they'd have it.

"This place is fucking creepy," Hawk whispered.

Cuckoo shrugged. "I kinda like it."

He would. Anything weird or horror-themed, he enjoyed. I hadn't noticed his costume until now. I'd been too distracted.

"Are you Indiana Jones?"

"It seemed appropriate," he answered with a shrug.

Claw snickered. "Yeah, it is, brother."

Earlier that day, I'd seen Cuckoo's prisoner costume and the shrunken heads on his belt. Now, he switched out his jeans for khaki pants and wore his cut over a brown leather jacket. It didn't make sense, but neither did Cuckoo half the time. A coiled whip was attached to his belt. He even wore a brown fedora like Indiana always had in the movies. For once, there wasn't any blood on him. No vampire teeth, either.

"You almost look respectable," I mused.

Cuckoo shrugged. "I like to keep everyone guessing."

"What's in the bag?" I asked, looking at the prop messenger bag he'd draped across his shoulder.

"Dynamite and snacks."

I pinched the bridge of my nose. "Let's keep moving."

Another long, mournful howl like the one we heard before we entered this forest echoed from somewhere ahead of us.

"Bella," I whispered, running in that direction, only to burst from the line of trees and enter a clearing with tall grass that reached my hip. Anything could be concealed here—even wolves.

"Shit, pres." Hawk ticked his chin. "We're goin' in blind."

"We move slow. Stay close," I ordered.

I noticed movement to our right and paused. Something scurried along the ground. We moved in that direction only to startle a flock of geese. They flew upward, honking and cackling as they took to the air, immediately flying in formation.

"Christ." Claw scrubbed a hand down his face. "Fucking geese."

"Be glad it wasn't a bear," Hawk joked.

Yeah. Wolves probably weren't the only predator in a hundred acres of forest. After Gail found the deed, I looked at a map of Undertaker's land. The forest was dense in spots. I knew Lake Alpine was remote enough to work for Undertaker's pack. They had the advantage of knowing the terrain.

We were too fucking vulnerable.

"Head to the trees."

We re-entered the forest, trying to keep track of the ground we already covered. Hawk used a compass on his phone. The more we walked, the deeper into the forest we traveled.

I stopped with a sigh. "Undertaker is toying with us."

"We're gonna end up lost," Claw agreed.

"What do you want to do, pres?"

I could feel eyes on us. The Dirty Death was out there. They were tracking our movements. Undertaker held them off. But why? And for how long?

56

"We need water," Cuckoo announced. He pulled a couple of canteens out of his bag.

"And to track Bella. She's the priority." My ol' lady was intelligent and resourceful. She'd get to a water source, too. Maybe she was at the lake, hiding and waiting for me to find her. It was worth a shot. "We get to the lake and look for any sign that Bella has been there."

I refused to believe that she was dead. Undertaker wanted me here. It didn't make sense to harm my woman. He wanted to maintain control, and he did as long as she was alive. The second she was harmed, that ceased to be his advantage. We both knew only bloodshed would follow.

He didn't kidnap her to kill her. He could have accomplished that without bringing her four hundred and fifty miles away to his pack land. The ancestral land he loved. No, he wanted that fucking deed and Bella was his insurance that he'd get it back, which proved this hunt was nothing more than a ruse. A distraction. He was playing a game.

For his pack members? Were they bored? Restless?

This grew tiresome. I didn't come all this way to hike through the fucking forest and delay finding Bella.

"Where are you, Undertaker?" I shouted. "Come out and stop hiding like a fucking coward!"

Only silence greeted me. Fuck!

We managed to find the lake an hour later. The surface glittered like thousands of clustered diamonds below the sun's bright rays. Crystal clear, blue-green waters were postcard-perfect, simply beautiful. The backdrop of lush green forest provided a view that dazzled the eye. It was the perfect escape from the world.

Bella had to be close.

We searched the embankment, following the lake's edge for miles. I had almost given up hope until I saw a pathway that dipped below a slab of overhanging rock.

It hid a rough trail that wrapped around the side of the lake and then led toward another section of forest.

My boots pounded the ground as I splashed through the shallow stream. There! Prints from a dainty pair of boots!

Baby, I'm here.

She walked through this path recently. The boot prints were still muddy and hadn't dried yet.

"Bella!"

BELLA

AS SOON AS I heard that howl, I knew the pack had found me.

In a futile effort, I ran. *Stupid.* I didn't make it far before I tripped over an exposed tree root. Not my finest or most graceful moment. I landed hard, twisting my ankle in the process.

"Fuck!" I screamed, blinking back tears. This wasn't good. Any second Dirty Death members would arrive. I was hurt and easy prey.

I rolled to my side and rose on my hands and knees. My ankle already throbbed, so I didn't think about anything other than getting back on my feet. I had to be strong. Fierce. Brave.

I used a nearby branch to steady myself as I slowly rose, testing my weight to see if I could stand on both feet.

Nope. I almost buckled with the wave of pain that followed.

Tears filled my eyes and spilled over. I swiped across my cheeks, hating feeling so weak and defeated. This wasn't how I was going to die. No fucking way. I'd come too far. I survived my parents' deaths, my Gram passing away, Bree's kidnapping and recovery, building my own business, and finally finding the perfect guy. It wouldn't end here.

I heard rustling and the heavy thud of something large moving toward me. On instinct, I scanned the area around me for a weapon. A heavy, thick branch had fallen from a nearby tree a few feet away. It looked snapped off, but I didn't care. It would be sturdy enough to use for protection.

I just had to reach it.

There wasn't time to crawl to it. I had to walk. Five steps. I nearly screamed at the pain shooting up my leg as my weight put pressure on my swelling ankle. I reached the branch and collapsed, picking it up as whoever found me finally reached my location.

It wasn't Undertaker or any of his club members. No wolves or dangerous predators.

"Crow!" I shouted, dropping the heavy branch.

My hero rushed toward me, falling to his knees. His arms surrounded me, and it was all it took for me not to burst into tears.

"Babe. I got you. I'm here."

"You found me," I blubbered.

"Always, Bella, mine." He tilted my chin up, pressing a soft kiss to my lips. "Are you hurt?"

"My ankle. I twisted it."

A grim nod followed. "Let me see."

I leaned back as he lifted my foot, scowling at the injury.

"Call Falcon," Crow bellowed. "Tell him to get here as quick as he can. We'll find him on the way back to The Roost."

I didn't notice Hawk, Claw, and Cuckoo were with him. "Hey, guys."

"Glad to see you, Bella," Hawk replied before he walked a short distance away, dialing Falcon's number.

Claw grinned. "You're tough."

"I had to be," I pointed out. "Big forest and all that."

Cuckoo patted me on the head. "You're hard to kill. That's good."

Nice. "I'm happy to see you all too."

"Bella." My name left Crow's lips in an agonized whisper. "I'm sorry I wasn't there. For our date. To protect you. If I had been," he began.

No. It wasn't his fault. "Hey. This isn't on you. I know what's going on with the club and all the shit with Undertaker. With Rook. I don't blame you."

"I could have lost you." His forehead lowered to mine. "Fuck, babe."

"I knew you would come. I never doubted."

His hand slid around my neck. The warmth of his fingers caressed my chilled skin. "Always."

"I think you need to marry me now," I joked.

"Bella, baby, that's my fucking goal. You say the date, and we will." His gaze locked on mine as he lifted his head. "I'm fucking serious."

"I know."

"Then when?"

"Next month. End of July."

"It's a date."

Chapter 9

UNDERTAKER

Sadie returned to me.

I knew the moment she set foot back on pack lands. Her delicate, sweet scent grew stronger and drifted in the wind, tickling my nose. More than that, I felt her presence. My wolf recognized his mate. The vargulf salivated at the thought of fucking her again.

My reaction was instant. A hard-on that could hammer nails.

But Sadie wasn't alone. She brought Carson, that fucking warlock. And those goddamn crows were here.

I shoved to my feet, knowing it was time to confront my enemy and that wasn't the president of the Devil's Murder MC. Although, he would definitely disagree.

The vargulf's days were numbered. I'd see to that. If I died, so be it. It was worth it to save my mate. We discussed this. She knew my wishes. Nothing mattered but saving her and making all the shit right that the vargulf had fucked up.

The pack had been unleashed to hunt but with strict guidelines: no harming Bella or the Devil's Murder members. They could intimidate, scare, or whatever else they wanted as long as they didn't touch them.

I knew they needed to run. Their wolves were restless. Tensions ran high. The vargulf had grown impatient and insatiable. I constantly battled his will. The result was a leader who seemed at war within himself, which caused confusion within the pack.

Someone would challenge me to lead soon. I'd have to rip out his throat. I didn't want to spill the blood of my brethren. The vargulf was unfazed by it—another reason he had to be put down. No leader should enjoy the thought of killing his clan, especially the Alpha.

Sadie would meet me at our favorite spot. In the late hours of the night, when the vargulf slept, I took her to the waterfall and bathed with her in the moonlight. There, exposed to the stars, we kissed and shared secrets.

I lost my heart to her in those precious stolen moments. Me. The vicious, ruthless monster. The murderous president of the Dirty Death MC. A man who never dared to dream of redemption. And she'd given me her trust.

For that reason alone, I knew Sadie would come.

Howls from the pack occasionally filled the forest as I walked to the waterfall, eager to see my mate. The vargulf seemed confused when I stopped here, fighting against my will. Over recent weeks, I had grown stronger while he'd grown weaker. The Alpha dominated the vargulf often.

He couldn't make me fuck or kill now at his whim.

Sadie's soft voice pulled me from my thoughts. "Undertaker."

I hated that name. The vargulf. What he represented. All that he'd done. "Sadie." I turned to her, noticing the healthy glow to her skin, the fresh flush in her cheeks, and the extra heartbeat thrumming inside her. Oh. Wow.

"You're pregnant." I dropped to my knees. "Beloved."

A brilliant smile lit up her beautiful face. "You dominated him." She meant the Alpha wolf had done it, not the vargulf.

"Yes. It's not without difficulty."

She turned to Carson, who stood beside her, poised to unleash his magic. I didn't blame him for feeling protective when I felt the same.

"We can still save him." She sent a pleading look to Carson. "Please."

He dropped his chin. "I'll try."

"That's all I can ask."

"My Sadie. It has to be done. When the time comes, don't hesitate." She knew what I meant. Only my death would leave the vargulf vulnerable enough to be killed.

Sudden tears filled her eyes. "What if I can't?"

"Then he will."

Carson sighed. "Yeah. I will."

"I know what you are," I told him. "How you hunt the vargulf. It's in your blood."

"For generations," he confirmed. "But we always failed. Until now."

I nodded. "Sadie."

She walked closer even when Carson tried to grab her arm. "No. He won't hurt me."

"I don't like it."

"It's not your choice."

"Fuck," Carson cursed, releasing her.

She approached me unafraid, and I lifted my hand, brushing my knuckles across the smooth, flawless skin of her cheek. "Do you remember?"

My name. I'd given it to her. The Alpha's *real* name.

"Yes."

"Good." I needed to kiss her one more time before it all went to shit. "A kiss to seal our promise."

She lifted her face, receiving my kiss with a passion that ignited my lust and fogged my brain. Sadie held a power over me no other being ever could. My mate could destroy or save me. It was her choice.

The crows didn't understand our ways. Crow didn't see the sacrifice of an Alpha. How much I would give up for Sadie.

That was why I used the magic of a witch to banish them from my lands. No fucking crows. The vargulf was pleased with himself for thinking of it.

Sadie wrapped her arms around me and hugged my waist. I didn't hesitate to enclose her in my embrace. My head lowered, and I inhaled her scent. For a few seconds, everything was right. Perfect. As close as I'd ever get.

I pressed a hand against her stomach. "I'm so fucking happy. Are you?"

"Yes."

"Tell him about me. I don't want him to learn only the bad. My legacy should be more than the vargulf."

"He'll know about *you*," she assured me.

That had to be enough. We were wasting time. I dropped my hand and took a few steps away from Sadie. I held her gaze, preparing for the vargulf's response. "Do it."

BELLA

"WE'RE ALMOST BACK TO the SUV," Crow assured me before kissing my temple. "Just a few more minutes."

"You sure you're okay to keep carrying me?"

He scoffed. "Babe. You aren't heavy."

"Yeah, but we've been walking for hours."

Cuckoo snorted. "I checked my phone. It's been forty-five minutes."

I lifted my middle finger and flipped him off.

"So feisty."

"No. I'm hangry, tired, and my ankle hurts." All legit reasons to be grumpy.

"Give her food," Crow ordered. "You said you had snacks."

Cuckoo opened his messenger bag and pulled out red licorice strips, Smarties, barbecue chips, and a granola bar. "What do you want?"

Crow growled. "Didn't you bring anything with protein?"

"I've got Snickers."

"Christ," he muttered. "Babe, I'll feed you once we're on the road."

I kissed his jaw. "Okay. For now, I want the Snickers."

Cuckoo handed the candy bar over, and I unwrapped it, chewing as my stomach rumbled.

"Is there anything to drink?"

"Gatorade. Here."

"Finally," Crow muttered. "Something that makes sense."

"I pride myself on being unpredictable," Cuckoo defended.

"And you are," Hawk agreed.

"Thanks, man."

Claw snickered. "Ain't ever boring with you guys."

Truth.

"We haven't heard any howls in a long while," Hawk observed after we walked a few more minutes in silence.

"I don't like it." Crow adjusted his hold. "What's the compass say? How close are we?"

"Maybe fifteen minutes. Hard to say."

"Why?"

"Because we're walking a bit slower now, pres."

Hawk was right. I slowed them down. At least, I did with Crow.

"Sorry, but not sorry," I sort of apologized. "It's my ankle's fault."

"Don't you be sorry, Bella. You're good, babe."

A sudden chorus of howls shattered the calm. They overlapped, growing higher in pitch, angrier, and more frantic. The forest seemed to shudder in response.

"Shit!"

"Fuck, pres!"

"Run!" Crow yelled, ordering Claw, Cuckoo, and Hawk to get their asses moving.

I jostled in Crow's arms and buried my face in his neck, trying to be as least cumbersome as I could.

The noise startled birds, and they flew into the air. Chaos seemed to ensue around us. I heard growls, too.

What was happening? Was it us? Or something else?

I could swear I felt hot breath on the back of my neck, and it wasn't from Crow.

We made it to the SUV, and Hawk opened the door as Crow reached it. I was settled on the seat as he climbed in beside me.

"We can't wait long for Carson and Sadie."

Wait. Were they here, too?

My gaze swept over the area outside the SUV and landed on the boulders and tunnel that marked the entrance to the jail cells. Oh. Shit. Rebel!

I couldn't leave her here.

"Babe. I need your help with something."

He reached for my hand. "Anything."

"I met someone when Undertaker put me in his dungeon. At least, I think it might have been a dungeon. It's not important." I sighed. "There's a girl in one of the cells. Her name is Rebel. She's a prisoner, too. We can't leave her there."

"No," he growled. "We can't."

He ticked his chin at Hawk. "Go."

"Wait!" Claw yelled, stepping up to Crow. "Send me, pres."

Crow relented. "Fine. Release anyone you find. No one deserves to be kept behind bars and subjected to Undertaker's sick pleasure."

Claw turned to me. "Where?"

"See those rocks? There's a set of concrete stairs. Follow them down."

"On it," he shouted, running in that direction.

"What's the plan, pres?"

"We stay here. Guard the SUV. Be ready for trouble."

"What about Carson and Sadie?" Cuckoo asked, withdrawing his gun.

"We wait until the last possible second. I don't want to leave them stranded."

Cuckoo and Hawk nodded, taking defensive positions outside the SUV. Crow shut the door. He held his Glock in one hand, ready to use it.

"Why are Carson and Sadie here?"

"Because Carson is working a spell on Undertaker. I want him unconscious so I can take him back to The Roost."

Oh, shit. "Revenge for Rook?"

"The club deserves it. It's their choice. I'm giving them the fucking option."

I didn't doubt Undertaker deserved everything he had coming to him. This still felt kinda wrong. "Will the crows attack him?"

"Probably, but not before every member of the club gets their turn first."

That sounded. . . bloody.

"So Carson isn't just a federal agent, huh?" I knew that. It had been hinted at. But no one thought to fill me in with all the recent shit that had gone down. Gail just got to The Roost. Talon was tortured by Undertaker and almost didn't make it. Laurel, Crow's mother, decided to pop into his life out of nowhere. It wasn't like he didn't have a ton of shit going on.

"Damn, babe. I didn't mean to exclude you."

"I know," I admitted truthfully.

"He's a warlock. Yeah. Crazy, right? He uses earth magic or some shit. He can help with the vargulf."

The vargulf. That was the darkness I felt around Undertaker.

"But he's not just a murderous beast. He's also an Alpha wolf. His clan's leader."

Wait. "He's two beings in the same body?"

"Yeah. It complicates everything."

I'd say so.

"These two parts," I wondered. "Is one good and one bad?"

He blinked. "I guess so. That's what Sadie says. The vargulf murdered Rook. He's raped, murdered, kidnapped, and tortured people. He sent Chronos to pick up Bree."

"Shit," I whispered.

"But the Alpha wolf, he's different. Arrogant. Lethal. Cunning. I can sense all those things about him. But he doesn't feel evil like the vargulf."

"I don't know if I can separate the two," I admitted truthfully. "Not after what happened to my sister."

"Then you know why I have to have justice and vengeance for my father."

I did.

"It still feels weird, doesn't it?"

He lifted a hand to cradle the side of my face. "Yes. Because you're not a cold-blooded killer. You have compassion."

A shout drew our attention as Claw ran toward the SUV. I saw Rebel behind him, along with two others—all women.

What the fuck, Undertaker?

Claw opened the side door, and the women climbed in. He then clicked the door shut behind them.

I turned to Rebel. "Hey. You okay?"

"We will be now."

I waved at the other two girls: a redhead and a brunette.

"Fuck," Crow growled.

I turned, catching Sadie as she ran toward us. Carson was dragging Undertaker by the boots!

Hawk, Claw, and Cuckoo rushed to help.

I wasn't sure how they managed to shove that big man into the SUV with us. Undertaker ended up in the back, and the vehicle sagged under his weight.

"Why is he with us?" Rebel asked, looking pissed.

"He's magically subdued," Carson promised as he sat behind the wheel, throwing it in drive.

Around us, howls split the air. The pack was converging.

Honestly, I thought they would have arrived sooner, but seeing Undertaker unconscious, I could guess why they got riled up.

We had to get out of here!

Carson sped away as over a dozen wolves exited the forest. He pushed down on the gas, lurching the vehicle as we passed through the main gate. I noted it had been destroyed, like someone had demolished it.

Damn. They bulldozed through it on the way in.

I watched as the wolves gave chase, but they weren't as fast. We left them behind as I sank into Crow's embrace.

"You're safe now, Bella. We'll handle the wolves once we're home."

I rested my head on his shoulder and yawned. I needed a nap.

There wasn't a better place in the world to fall asleep than in his arms. He slid an arm around me, and I snuggled close, too exhausted to fight it.

Chapter 10

BELLA

"I NEED A SHOWER," I announced as we entered our upstairs apartment at The Roost. It had been a long and exhausting car ride, and I rested as often as I could, but it was challenging with all the conversation on the way back. I couldn't even think of all that now.

Falcon met us halfway through the trip home, and he healed my ankle, promising I would feel better soon. He wasn't lying. I hardly noticed the injury now. It was tender and sore but no longer painful to walk.

"C'mon, babe. I'll take care of you."

Crow led me to the bathroom and carefully undressed me, holding me against his side as he turned on the water and tested the temperature. The man knew exactly what I liked. He was a keeper.

Not to mention, he risked his life for me—more than once. I stepped inside as he undressed, standing under the spray for a couple of minutes without moving. The hot water soothed my aching muscles and helped relax them.

"Let me lather you," Crow offered as I nodded.

He poured some of my shampoo into his palm, and I moved to give him better access. His fingers massaged my scalp as he washed my hair, and it was heaven.

"You keep moaning like that, and I'm gonna think it's an invitation for more."

"Always sex on your brain."

"With you, babe? Hell yeah."

I rinsed the soap and applied conditioner, laughing as he soaped up my loofa.

His brows wiggled. "I'm gonna wash you thoroughly now."

"Uh-huh."

I was confident that Crow had magic fingers, even more so than Falcon when it came to knowing my body. The man had a tender yet bold touch. He caressed and stroked my skin as need darkened his eyes.

I tilted my head back when he began to wash my breasts, rinsing off the soap and replacing the loofa with his tongue. He teased each nipple, sucking and licking until I squirmed.

Crow lowered to his knees. His hands dipped to caress my inner thighs. He let his fingers wander close to my center. Such a tease. He lifted one of my legs, placing it over his shoulder. "Brace yourself, my love."

His love. Crow had called me a wide variety of endearments since we began dating but never that one. God, I loved him so much it made my heart ache. I didn't know you could feel this happy or fulfilled with another person.

"I mean it. Everything I said. Marry you. Spend my life with you. Fucking you. A lot. Tasting this pussy. All of it."

"I believe you."

"You're my favorite narcotic."

"Oh, you do drugs now?"

He smirked. "Just you, babe. I'll take a shot of you into my veins as often as I can. Overdose on your sweet pussy. I'm addicted."

I couldn't hold back a slight chuckle. "Is that so?"

"You paralyze me, Bella. Can't fight my craving for you."

"Yeah? I feel the same."

He leaned forward and swiped his tongue between my legs, never breaking eye contact. "You taste like heaven."

"Then I guess I'm an angel."

We had the silliest banter during sex. I loved it.

"I'm so fucking hard right now."

"Then why aren't you inside me, Austin?"

He shook his head. "Not yet."

His lips latched onto my clit, and I bucked my hips as two of his thick fingers entered me. I was already wet, and he growled with approval. He slowly pumped in and out of me, increasing in speed, and building up my orgasm.

Crow knew how to get me off and didn't waste time. I came with a shudder as he lapped at my pussy. I nearly fell over when he stood.

A smile teased his lips as he licked them and pressed my back against the wall, holding me upright. "Babe. I need your pussy now. Tell me to fuck you."

"Oh, God. Give it to me good, Crow."

His hands gripped my waist and lifted me as I wrapped my legs around his torso, admiring all the firm muscle. He had abdominal muscles that would make a bodybuilder jealous. The perfect grooves on the sides of hips. The kind of physique women went wild over, and he was all mine.

Not to mention, Crow had a big, thick cock. The full package.

He stroked his erection with one hand, his other holding my ass for support. "You want this dick, baby?"

"Yes!"

Laughter rumbled through his chest. "You sound impatient. Didn't you just come on my tongue?"

Yeah. So? "Please," I begged.

He notched the crown at my entrance and plunged inside me in a swift, deep thrust. I cried out as he moved, snapping his hips hard and fast. At this angle, my body weight and gravity pushing me down on him, I could feel him hitting that perfect spot. The one that always made me come hard and soak him.

He knew that.

"Play with your clit. This isn't going to be a slow, lazy fuck. I'll make love to you later, babe. Right now, I need to feel you squeeze my dick and come all over it."

And I did. My whole body trembled with my orgasm, and I gripped his shoulders, bouncing on his cock. Jesus. I almost shoved him out of me, I clenched him so hard.

"Fuck, babe. Fuck!"

Crow shuddered as his hips drove me into the wall. He lasted a few more deep strokes and stilled. "I think I just made you dirty again."

"Should we check?"

"Fuck yeah." He slowly withdrew, his cock still hard and bobbing between us.

Fluids dripped from my pussy.

"Goddamn. It turns me on to see my cum drip out of you."

"Best two out of three?" I asked, licking my lips.

"I might need motivation. My cock is tired."

Yeah. Right. "Well, I can play with my pussy and our cum while I suck your dick."

A growl left his throat before his mouth captured mine. The kiss was sensual and slow, a contradiction to how we just fucked. I loved that.

Sex was always enjoyable with Crow. We kept it spicy and spontaneous.

The shower had grown cold by the time we left it.

Crow dried me off and carried me to bed. "Rest. I'll be back soon."

"President stuff," I whispered with a yawn.

"Yeah, Bella, mine. Love you, gorgeous."

I think I replied, but I couldn't be sure.

CROW

BELLA FELL ASLEEP ALMOST as soon as her head rested on the pillow. I stared down at her, watching the serene expression on her face. She never said she was scared when Undertaker's club kidnapped her, but I was sure she had felt that way. It pissed me off that she'd been hungry, alone, and wandering a forest with no way to know if or when she would be rescued.

She believed in me and trusted me to rescue her, but that didn't erase the trauma.

"I'll take care of this," I whispered. "Love you, Bella, mine."

I posted a prospect outside my door and told him not to move. I wasn't leaving her unprotected again.

Raven met me at the bottom of the stairs. "Pres. What's on the agenda?"

"Gather everyone outside."

He nodded, hollering at members to drop what they were doing and head toward the lot. We had about a dozen guys around the perimeter of our compound to watch for trouble from the wolves. Undertaker's club could attack any moment, and I prepared the club for lash back.

"Crow. You still need us?" Rael asked, approaching with Exorcist and Patriot.

They had arrived during our absence when I went after Bella. I appreciated them waiting and enjoying our hospitality until we were ready to deal with Undertaker.

Raven and Patriot hugged. Their friendship ran deep and stemmed from Raven's days in the military when he served with Patriot's older brother.

"I do. There's a vargulf that needs a reaping."

His grin widened. It might not be weird, except for the fact that Rael never went anywhere without his makeup. Black and white face paint depicted a skull on his face with blacked-out eyes and nose. The fucker was creepy as hell but loyal.

I trusted all the Tonopah Royal Bastards. Grim and my pops were close. Our clubs partied and shared members when in need. And today, I needed their unique ability.

There was a reason they were called reapers. We were crows, able to shift, control, and bond with our black feathered birds. The reapers were grims, and they had the spiritual ability to reap the souls of the wicked. It was fucking frightening but badass.

"A vargulf?" Exorcist asked. "Damn. That's a new one."

"Mark it on our list of dead fuckers we've sent to Lucifer," Rael laughed.

Damn. That was a morbid thought.

Patriot ticked his chin at me. "He deserve this?"

"He does. It's Rook's murderer."

They all stiffened.

"Done," Rael announced.

"He'll fucking suffer," Patriot added.

"There's one complication," Raven informed them.

"We're attempting to separate the vargulf from his host."

Exorcist frowned. "His host?"

"Yeah," I answered. "The vargulf is evil. He's taken over the pack's Alpha. Yeah, it was his fucking choice, but I don't think he knew how fucking evil that thing was when he let it bond with him."

"So you're trying to save one being and reap the other?" Rael clarified.

"That's the gist."

"Complicated. I like it."

"We've never done anything like this. I think Lucifer will enjoy this vargulf. He'll have fun with such a creature," Exorcist mused.

Carson entered the bar, and I waved him over. "This is Carson. He's a warlock."

The reapers looked surprised.

"I know. There's too much spiritual shit going on around here lately. But Carson is our secret weapon other than you lot."

Rael snickered.

Carson nodded to Rael, Exorcist, and Patriot. He glanced over their cuts and read each name. "I've got a spell I can use. It's a little complex, but what you all need to know is that this is going to happen quickly. We have a small window."

Patriot crossed his arms over his chest. "For what?"

"The reaping. When I begin the spell, it will agitate the vargulf. He'll get pissed because I'm going to make it really fucking uncomfortable to stay with the Alpha."

"Good," Rael grunted.

"But there's a chance he won't leave the host. If he doesn't, we'll have to reap both souls together. The vargulf can't be allowed to survive. Not after all he's done."

"I don't want to clarify, but the vargulf has killed, beaten, kidnapped, and raped numerous individuals. And he took my father from me," I snarled, "So he fucking goes to Lucifer. There's no choice in that."

Rael, Patriot, and Exorcist agreed.

Raven gripped my shoulder. "We'll finally get justice and closure."

"And there's no turning back. We do this in front of the club. If they want to take hits, we let them. We just can't let the Alpha die before the vargulf is sent to hell."

Sadie walked from the kitchen as I spoke those last words. "No. Please, Crow."

"You're not gonna like it, Sadie, but this is our way. It's final."

She blinked back tears. "But the Alpha, he's good. He doesn't deserve to die."

"Then you need to convince him to push out the vargulf because the club won't let that slide. That evil fuck is going down. I won't let another moon rise before my father is vindicated."

Sadie sniffled. "I understand. I'll do everything I can to help."

"Good," Raven answered, "because I have a feeling it's going to be you that settles this."

With the plan in place, we all left the bar at peace with our decision.

Chapter 11

CROW

"YOU ALL KNOW WHY we've gathered. It's been too fucking long, but we're finally getting justice for Rook," I announced.

Cheers erupted from several club members. Others swore a bloody end to the asshole who hurt Rook.

Undertaker was brought to the corner of the lot outside our workshop. I had him chained to a couple of steel beams, arms spread apart, and legs kicked wide. He formed an X in front of the crowd. His body had been pulled tight, and he'd withstand whatever beating the club decided to give him.

I glanced at his face, nothing the absence of emotion. It was hard to tell if the vargulf or the Alpha was in control. I hoped the vargulf because this wasn't going to be pretty. "Raven. You're up."

My V.P. and Rook's best friend approached from the right. He didn't say shit to Undertaker before he swung his fist, landing a punch to his gut that I knew had to hurt.

Undertaker grunted. That was it.

Raven jabbed at his jaw and stomach a few times before spitting at his chest. "Fuck you for taking our president. Go to hell."

A few members grew vocal, agreeing with Raven.

"Hawk."

Our S.A.A. got his hits in next, using his kickboxing skills to full effect. I don't think my fucking balls would withstand that kind of attack.

"Talon."

I called up members one by one. They all took their turn, exacting justice with violence. That was our way of honoring Rook and letting the past go. We had to make peace with it, heal, and move on as a club.

When I took my turn, I pulled a knife. I needed to spill his blood. The first slice unleashed my fury. The fifth finally gave me clarity. By the time I held the blade to his throat, I felt free.

Undertaker dangled by the chains, a bloody, swollen, disfigured lump of flesh when I backed away. I heard a couple of bones crack during this process. He had a black eye that darkened more with every passing second. Split lip. Bruises. Burns. Cuts. Blood-soaked clothes. A Lot of members spit on him. A couple pissed on him. He fucking stunk.

I almost opened my mouth to tell Carson to begin the spell when the flapping of wings caught my attention. And from the shadows, with a crow perched on each shoulder, Carrion joined us—the last to serve judgment.

"They're ready now," he murmured.

Well, damn. Crows flew in from all directions. They perched on the roof and dropped to the asphalt, hopping as they cawed. I watched as they formed a mobbing, furious as they continued to squawk and chitter, berating Undertaker for taking Rook from us. A sea of black blinked around us, calming as I heard a single flap of wings.

One lone crow.

A bird I knew as well as my own, but I hadn't seen him or felt his presence since my father's death.

Rook's crow.

My club brothers fell silent. Some lowered their heads.

I couldn't help watching him approach.

Rook's crow dove for me and landed on my shoulder. "Kraa."

I couldn't have said it better myself.

Carrion cleared his throat. "He came one last time for Rook."

Fuck. I promised myself I wouldn't cry.

A dark laugh erupted from Undertaker. "Quite a show. But I don't think you considered that wolves can break steel." He snapped the chains that bound him, swinging his arms as he bounded toward me.

I turned to Carson. "Now!"

We anticipated something like this. The vargulf didn't care if the Alpha was injured. He could heal. Wolves had that ability to a certain extent. Beating him would do nothing to the vargulf. I had to let the club have its vengeance before I could finish with our plan.

Carson lifted his hands as a dark red fog began to slowly leave his fingertips. It traveled on a current of soundless wind, swirling in front of Undertaker a second before it launched toward him. The red fog penetrated his eyes, nose, and mouth. It invaded his ears, sinking into his skin and entering his body.

Undertaker began to convulse. His body shook, gyrating as the spell's power surrounded the dark entity inside the Alpha.

But the vargulf wasn't going to leave that easily. I knew that. He roared as he fought the red fog, punching at the air. He hissed and snarled. Somehow, he seemed to grow in size. Inches added to his height. His bulky frame widened.

"Rael!" I called next, bringing in the reapers.

The ground rumbled beneath my feet as Rael, Exorcist, and Patriot transformed into their grims. Their bodies took on the skeletal form of the reaper, cloaked in black. Rising above the ground, they hovered in a macabre trio, suspended in the air as an invisible wind billowed their onyx robes.

My club members stared with curiosity. Most hadn't seen a reaping before now.

In each hand of the reapers, a deadly scythe appeared. I gulped when I noticed that each sickle gleamed and dripped with blood. Faceless forms seemed to cry out in agony within the blades. They swayed and moved as if in torment and couldn't stop.

Christ. That was unnerving.

The ground shook again as the crows lifted, giving space to the grims and fissures that cropped up. They tore apart the asphalt and rock, busting the dirt until the cracks gave way and the hole opened wider. Hellfire streamed from the massive crater, opening a one-way ticket to hell.

The vargulf increased his struggles. He howled as he fought, unable to move from his position. "I will take him with me!" He roared.

Sadie ran forward, but Carson grabbed her around the waist.

"Alpha!" Her voice sounded frantic.

"You will be the first to die, bitch!"

The vargulf was a nasty fucker.

"Let him go. Please!"

"No!" The vargulf wouldn't relent. He was too filled with hate to see that Sadie was motivated by love.

And that was his mistake.

"Caden," she whispered. "Come to me."

Caden. The Alpha's real name. Sadie fulfilled her vow.

A horrendous cry launched from the vargulf's mouth as he opened wide, black sludge spewing from his gullet. It splashed onto the ground, spilling from the Alpha's body. He shook and jolted, ejecting more of that blackened sputum until nothing more came out. The Alpha, Caden, collapsed. He no longer hosted the vargulf.

The black sludge bubbled and hissed. It began to take shape, forming into the body of a beast. Wolf-like, it rose off the ground on two clawed feet, bellowing in rage.

He didn't have time to do a thing before the reapers attacked.

The scythes cut through the vargulf's form, slashing and hacking at the onyx filth. It tore apart like flesh, bleeding with a pus-like texture. The stench of sulfur almost made my stomach retch.

Around us, outside the compound, howls rose in unison, a chorus of wolves that had come for their Alpha. But they weren't attacking. I caught the glowing eyes that watched. Maybe they also wished for the vargulf to die.

The vargulf's putrid essence began to fall into the abyss, slowly dropping into the hellfire that popped and hissed. I could swear that it seemed to gobble up those tainted remnants and swallow them down, dropping the vargulf's body piece by piece into Lucifer's domain.

When none remained, the fissures closed. The ground smoothed out. Crows took to the air, cawing and cackling in victory. Around our compound, the wolves' howls joined in the celebration. The vargulf had been defeated.

The reapers lowered beside me, and their dark cloaks, skeletal faces, and scythes disappeared. Rael, Patriot, and Exorcist appeared the same as they had before the reaping. Looking at them, you would never know what they hid inside. Well, except for maybe Rael. That fucker was too goddamn nuts to hide shit.

I still liked him. Somewhat.

Carson released Sadie, and she ran to Caden, hugging him as he groaned. His battered body needed a healer.

"Falcon!" I hollered.

"On it, pres. Without that evil thing inside him, I don't mind."

Not a soul disagreed.

"Caden," Sadie sobbed.

"I'll heal," he groaned. "Promise, my mate."

"I can help speed it along if you want," Falcon offered.

"You won't mind?"

"You're no longer the vargulf, right?"

"Yeah."

"You gonna hurt anyone here?"

"Of course not."

"Then let me heal you and stop jabbering."

Caden laughed. "Alright."

Falcon's touch spawned immediate improvement. The bruises began to fade. The busted lip smoothed, and the blood stopped dripping from his wounds. Caden sat up, grinned, and finally stood. He cracked his neck and rolled his shoulders. Within a few minutes, it never looked as if he'd taken such a brutal beating.

I had to say, the guy handled it bravely. He wasn't a pussy.

"Thank you. All of you." He reached out for Sadie and brought her close. "I can be with my mate and child now. I didn't dare to hope it would be possible after all the vargulf had done. You've given me a chance at a new beginning."

Sadie tilted his head down. "I love you."

They shared a kiss as Carson cleared his throat.

She held out her hand. "And you, also, Carson."

Caden turned to me. "The deed."

Yes. I knew he would want it. "You'll be in a contract with me to pay back the money, but the land is yours. I don't need or want it. Rook never did. He only wanted to bargain for the vargulf to leave our club alone and drop his vendetta."

"I don't know if I could be as generous and forgiving as you."

"You would have. We both want the same thing. Our women, club, and peace."

"You're right."

I handed over the deed as Caden opened his mouth and howled. His pack joined him.

I turned to the Devil's Murder, finally feeling free. On the faces of my club members, I found the same burden had been lifted. Rook had been avenged, and our enemy vanquished.

This was a good fucking day.

Chapter 12

UNDERTAKER

"WHAT WILL YOU DO now?" Crow asked.

We had gathered in The Roost's bar. Seated at a table, I shared a drink with men I no longer considered enemies. It was such a bizarre but welcome twist that I felt gratitude and relief that the vargulf's presence was gone.

I tightened my hold around Sadie as she sat on my lap, nuzzling her neck before I lifted my head to answer. "A few things, including some major housecleaning," I joked.

Chuckles erupted around the table.

"But first order of business, I'll meet with my club and bring a vote to the table for a name change."

Crow nodded. "A wise decision. You got an idea what you want to use?"

"I do," I admitted. "Night Striders MC."

"I like it. It works with the whole wolf thing."

"It does," I laughed.

"I'm glad you survived the reaping." Raven slapped my back. "It was a little touch and go there for a minute."

No shit. "Yeah. It hurt like a motherfucker."

Crow snorted.

"But that reaping? A fucking beautiful thing to watch," I admitted.

Rael grinned. "I knew I liked you, you crazy wolf."

"Alpha," I corrected.

"Alpha Caden," Sadie murmured.

"All yours," I replied, kissing her again. I couldn't seem to stop.

It was strange not to feel the heavy, oppressive presence of the vargulf. He'd been a part of me for so long that it felt too bright and happy now. Like I could pinch myself and wake up from a dream. It had an element of fantasy that spooked me.

I never wanted to live in that darkness again. There was so much to do now. So many things to make right. The vargulf had torn my pack apart, caused dissension, and messed with the hierarchy. I had to fix those things, and they would take time.

But I wasn't doing this alone. I had my mate. My Sadie. And with the birth of my heir, the pack would heal from the rifts of our past. The damage that had become a stain on our clan would be cleansed. I would usher in a new era where the vargulf could no longer control or use my lineage.

"I got a question." Exorcist ticked his chin my way. "That vargulf thing. Can it come back? Try to corrupt the next generation?"

"No. I don't think so," I replied slowly, thinking it over.

I could see all the curious expressions and concern. They wanted reassurance this shit couldn't repeat.

"I once believed a new vargulf rose to power with the birth of every new generation, but I don't believe that now. It was the same evil entity seeking out each new Alpha. He deceived my family for many years."

"I'm glad we reaped that motherfucker," Rael sneered.

"Not more than me. I'm no longer a slave to his whim. I almost lost everything, including my mate and my pack. I'll stay vigilant, but I don't think there was more than the one vargulf. I've never heard of any beyond our lands."

Crow shoved a beer in my direction. "It's time we buried the past and toasted to our future. The sins of our fathers no longer tie us down, and neither do their mistakes or grudges."

"I'll drink to that."

He tapped his bottle to mine. "To a new dawn."

"And new beginnings."

CROW

"So," I SLIGHTLY SLURRED, "I'm gettin' married."

A few shouts erupted around me, and hands slapped my back. I nearly stumbled, drunk off my ass, after spending the last few hours with Caden, Rael, Exorcist, Raven, Talon, Hawk, and Patriot. After all the shit that had gone down, I needed something good in my life, and the club did too.

"Bella doesn't know it yet, but we're doing this on Saturday."

Fists pounded the tables. Laughter followed.

This felt right. Perfect. I needed my ol' lady as my wife.

"I'm plannin' this surprise, and you're all invited. So don't fuck it up and let her find out."

The bar had emptied of ol' ladies and sweet butts at this point. Only members continued the celebration late into the night. We would be worthless with the sunrise, hungover, and sleep deprived, but damn, this party was fuckin' awesome.

I took my seat, almost falling off as Raven shoved my shoulder, forcing me upright.

"What made you finally want to get hitched?" Rael asked.

"Found my forever in a tight pussy, pretty green eyes, and the only woman brave enough to order me around, and I liked it."

Yeah, I probably should have censored that.

Guffaws followed my words.

"Bella's good for you. Rook would have loved her," Raven informed me, gripping my shoulder. "About time you had some happiness."

Talon grinned. "The club respects her. She's tough."

"But she's sweet," Hawk added.

My Bella was the whole package.

I turned to Caden. "Tell me you're stickin' around for this."

He looked surprised. "I'd be honored."

Good. "How about Grim and the rest of the Royal Bastards?"

"Give him a call. We'll all show up and crash the party," Rael joked.

I'd do that. As soon as I wasn't so fucking drunk.

Exorcist smirked. "You gonna remember this conversation tomorrow?"

"Hell yeah." I reached into my pocket and showed them the engagement ring I bought Bella three months ago. "I haven't found the right moment to ask her until now."

Rael whistled. "Damn."

"That's a big fucking rock," Patriot laughed. "Good for you."

"I finally feel like I can put the past behind me and move forward." A smile lifted my lips as I stared at the ring. "I'm done holding onto the things I can't change. Time to build a future with my ol' lady."

"To you and Bella," Caden announced, lifting his beer.

My friends and brothers all repeated after him.

"To the club, resolved issues, and being fucking happy."

LOU NEARLY RAMMED HIS scooter into the table the following afternoon. "Heard you're plannin' to marry Bella."

"I am."

"Good. You got a ring? Let me see it."

I chuckled, pulling out the box and revealing it to him. "I've had it for three months."

He had his cane with him today, and he whacked my knee with it. "About damn time you made her honest. When is the ceremony?"

I rubbed my leg. "Damn. You tryin' to give me a bruise?"

"The ceremony?"

"Saturday at sunset. Here at The Roost."

Lou grinned. "You did good. She'll love it."

I knew that already.

"Tell her I'd be honored if she needs someone to walk her down the aisle."

Oh. Wow. "Thanks."

"Don't cry, boy. It's not a big deal."

We both knew it was huge. Bella and Bree's parents died when they were kids. They were raised by their Gram.

"I'll tell her."

"Who's catering?"

"Me." Bree overheard us as she left the kitchen. "I'm counting on you to help me, Lou."

He flashed a cheesy grin. "I'm on my way."

I had to move my feet or risk Lou running them over. He was a fucking danger in that scooter, and he loved it.

Gail entered the bar with Talon, and they joined me at the table. "You have anyone doing the flowers yet?"

Flowers? Shit. "Uh."

Gail giggled. "I thought so. I'm taking care of it."

"Thank fuck."

Talon cleared his throat. "Crow."

"We're good, Talon. But if you fuck this up with Gail, I will personally cut off your cock and watch you eat it."

Gail's jaw popped open.

Talon laughed. "Okay, pres. I love Gail. It won't be an issue."

"Then I have nothing to worry about."

I spotted Raven at the bar and excused myself, heading toward my V.P., the only man besides Lou I would consider for the most important day of my life.

"Hey," I greeted him.

"Pres."

"I got a serious question to ask you."

"Shoot."

"Would you be my Best Man?"

He blinked. The glass in his hand slipped from his fingers and landed on the bar with a splash. "I'd be honored, Austin."

"If my pops can't be here, you're the one I want standing up there with me."

"I wouldn't have it any other way."

He leaned in for a hug first, and of all the hugs I'd had recently, that was the one that brought tears to my eyes. Embracing Raven was like a part of me connecting with Rook.

This sure ended up being an emotional few days.

I dropped outside for a smoke and leaned against the exterior wall, slapping a cigarette from the pack into my palm. The temperature had cooled considerably after dusk, and I relaxed, relieved that no enemy lingered beyond these gates to cause trouble.

I heard the door open, and Patriot joined me. "Can we talk?"

"Sure, brother."

"You remember that I served overseas?"

"Yeah."

"Well, one of my fellow Marines had an interesting ability. I didn't find out about it until after I was honorably discharged."

I gave him my full attention. "A crow?"

"I believe so. He's got a son. Kid is twenty-two and fucking cocky. He needs guidance. I can't bring him in as a reaper, but I wondered if you'd meet. Size him up. See if he's a good fit for the Devil's Murder."

"What's his name?"

"Heron."

Heron? That was interesting.

"Set it up."

"I will."

Chapter 13

CROW

"Hey, Gail," I greeted my sister. "You got a minute?"

I had knocked on her door, conveniently at the apartment beside mine, with a nervous flutter in my stomach.

"Sure, Austin."

"I have something I want to show you."

She followed me back to my room, watching with curiosity as I sat behind my desk.

"This used to be Rook's desk. He loved to sit here and sort club business and his finances and sometimes just to think and get a few minutes to himself."

She smiled. "I like that. It was his spot."

"A favorite." I cleared my throat. "I had a hard time sitting here after his death. It felt wrong, just like parking my bike in his spot. It fucking hurt," I admitted, tapping my chest over my heart. "But I finally went through it a couple of days ago."

She blinked, and I could tell she was curious. "You found something, didn't you?"

"Yeah."

"Show me."

I pulled another chair close and gestured for her to sit.

Gail joined me. "It's a gorgeous desk."

"He had it custom-made. I never understood why until I accidentally unlocked a hidden compartment." I pressed the button that released the lock, and it popped open.

Gail gasped. "Wow."

"You wanna see what's in it?"

She nodded.

I reached inside, gathered all the newspaper articles, awards, photos, and memorabilia my father had compiled and placed them in Gail's hands.

Her gaze swept over the thick stack, and she cleared her throat. "Oh, Austin."

"If you want to look at this alone, I'm happy to leave you to it."

Gail shook her head. "No. I think I'd like you to stay."

So I did.

We took our time, reading through the articles and every award and talking about each photo. It took me a minute to notice her tears, and I slid an arm around her shoulders, squeezing her against my side.

"We had to spend a lot of our lives apart. I hate that, but I'm so happy we have a chance to make up for it now."

Gail sniffled. "Me too."

"Do you know why I wanted to show you all this?"

"I think so. I mean, I can guess."

"It's because you grew up with an asshole and he wasn't your dad. You didn't get to experience Rook as your father, but he loved you. The whole time growing up, you thought it was your Uncle Derek, but you had a father."

"Austin," she lifted her head, chin wobbling.

"Your father wanted to be part of your life, and he made sure he found a way to do it."

Tears spilled down her cheeks, and I held her as she sobbed, the pain of the past finding a way to bubble up and out of her to give my sweet sister the closure she needed.

It wasn't fair to her to learn about a father and to lose him at the same time. I wanted to be there for her to show her she wasn't alone. She still had family.

She smiled when her tears stopped and swiped them from her cheeks. "I needed that."

"I know."

"You know what?"

I shook my head.

"You're the best brother I could have ever hoped for, Austin. I love you."

Damn. That hit me right in the chest. "I love you, too."

Gail gathered everything into a neat stack and placed it back in the secret compartment. "It seems wrong to take it from here. I like knowing these things are where he wanted them, that he used to open that hidden drawer and look at them, thinking of me."

"I'm sure he did."

She leaned against me, and we sat in silence for a few minutes. It wasn't uncomfortable. I bet we both thought of Rook and tried our best to focus on the positive.

"I want to do something," I began, "and I'd like you to be part of it. In fact, I'm hoping you'll come with me since you already offered."

Gail straightened, looking up at me. "You want to talk to Laurel."

"I do. I think I need to since it's the last loose end of my past."

"It's a wise choice, Austin. I'm proud of you. I know it's not easy."

No. It was fucking hard.

"When do you want to go?"

"Give me an hour. I have to settle a few things, and then we'll leave."

She lifted up from the chair and kissed my cheek. "Done, big brother."

"ARE YOU READY?" GAIL asked, placing her hand over mine.

"I don't think I'll ever be fucking ready."

"We don't have to rush. Take all the time that you need."

"That's the thing," I sighed. "It's best just to rip off this bandaid."

"Alright. Let's go."

Gail didn't give me a chance to back out. She opened the car door and left her seat, leaning down to stare at me. "C'mon."

Funny how I could party with grim reapers, stare death in the face, confront a vargulf, and witness hell opening a gigantic fucking hole in my parking lot, but the idea of having this conversation with my mother scared me.

No. Not fear. A whole range of emotions.

Tension. Anxiety. Stress. Uncertainty. Anger. Betrayal. Hurt.

They all formed a heavy knot in my stomach.

"Austin."

"Fine," I grumbled, finally joining her. "She said it's room 315."

Gail nodded. "Okay."

We entered the hotel side by side, walking through the rows of slot machines to reach the elevator. Neither of us spoke much as we waited for the doors to open.

Gail reached for my hand and squeezed. Fuck. I squeezed back, and we dropped hands.

There wasn't any guarantee Laurel would be in her room, and I should have thought about that before we drove here. Maybe I should have called first. No. This needed to happen in person.

Her room was halfway down the hall on the right. I paused outside of it, rubbing my palms on the thighs of my jeans.

"Want me to knock?" Gail asked with a whisper.

I shook my head.

It was now or fucking never. I squared back my shoulders, lifted my hand, and knocked. Hard.

That should get her attention.

The door swung open almost right away. And there, in the doorway, stood Laurel.

"Hi. Come on in." She stood back, gesturing for us to enter. "There's a great balcony view outside the room. We can talk out there. If you want."

Gail smiled. "Sure."

I couldn't seem to speak, so I nodded.

My gaze bounced around her room. Tidy. Organized. She always kept a clean house when I was a kid.

We followed Laurel through the glass door, and she shut it behind us. The balcony was pretty, with plenty of plants and cozy furniture.

It didn't make a difference to me where my ass landed, but I appreciated the effort to make us comfortable. At least the effort for my sister.

Gail sat. Laurel sat in the chair beside her. I couldn't sit. Not yet.

"Austin, uh, Crow, I'm sure you have a lot of questions. Go ahead."

"Why now?" That was the first one. I couldn't figure out why the timing seemed so important. She could have come anytime in the last six months since Rook's death, but she chose now.

"Because that's when Carrion said you would listen." She smiled. "He also said to show you this." Laurel reached behind her chair and pulled out a big box. "Here."

Fuck. Carrion? Again? He spoke to Rook. He told him every step in the plan that led to the vargulf's capture and reaping. Did he talk to Laurel, too?

"Please," Laurel pleaded.

I reached for the box and balanced it on a nearby table. With my gut churning, I opened the lid and stared at its contents.

Jesus. Fucking. Christ.

I jumped back like I had been burned. My head suddenly pounded, and my heart raced. I shook my head. "No."

"It's everything I've gathered over the last eighteen years. Everything I could find about you, your club, and the things you love."

Oh. Fuck. Fuck!

Inside the box, eerily similar to the secret drawer where my father had kept all the memorabilia of Gail, Laurel had gathered her own cherished memories—all of me, her son.

"Austin," she croaked.

I was going to lose it. My hands clenched. My lungs ached.

For the first time since my father's death, a sob shook loose from my chest.

Gail stood, but she didn't rush toward me. She didn't need to. Comfort came from the one person in this world that I swore to forget. The woman who left and abandoned me. The mother who stained my life and my perception of women, relationships, and family.

I could still see her driving away in that taxi when I was seven years old, waving at her with a smile because I had no idea it was the last time I would see her for nearly two decades.

"Why do you have all this?" I managed to growl. Anger was the only emotion I could hold onto without falling apart.

Laurel approached, stopping a few inches away from me. "Because I never stopped loving you, caring about you, or wanting to be a part of your life."

No. Fuck. That couldn't be true. Right?

"Austin, look at me."

It took every ounce of courage I had to face her.

"I love you, son. I always have."

I shook my head hard.

"I left you because I had to do it, or you would have died. Your father and I made a plan. Someone had to sacrifice. Rook insisted he was the one. His blood for yours. He died to save us both."

Fuck. Fuck. Fuck.

How did I believe this? How could I trust her?

"Carrion said you would doubt so he told me what to say. He knew you would meet Bella, and the vargulf was a dangerous enemy. He would have taken Gail, harmed Bella, and destroyed your club."

So no witness protection or club rivalry to drive a wedge between Rook and Laurel?

"I had to leave Austin. I sacrificed my relationship with your father to ensure you lived."

It seemed too farfetched—too easy an explanation.

Why would she listen to Carrion? Or Rook about this? It was asking so much of her.

How could anyone walk away from their child like that?

"Austin," Gail whispered as she joined me, resting her head against my shoulder. "You came here for the truth. You can't decide it's a lie because it's hard to hear, big brother."

"It's too unbelievable to consider the truth."

"That's because your heart is hurting."

"Fuck, Gail."

"Think about Carrion. Would he do all of this to deceive you?"

"No," I exhaled.

She reached up and tapped the end of my nose. "Then there's your answer."

I had to take several deep breaths before I could face Laurel. I finally turned toward her, unsettled by the tears filling her eyes.

"I've waited so long for this day, son." Her voice broke. "Please forgive me." She opened her arms wide.

I've heard it said that the first step is always the hardest. Whoever phrased that wasn't lying. I moved toward my mother, and with every step, it got easier. More of my doubt crumbled away until I reached her.

When her arms surrounded me, I almost buckled. I didn't have a clue what kept me upright other than the thought I could crush her from my weight. She was tiny. Smaller than Gail or Bella.

"Austin."

"I forgive you."

I didn't say it for her, not really. I said those words for me because I realized I had held onto them for so fucking long.

They festered inside me. I allowed those negative emotions to control me. Not after today.

In that moment, I came to the conclusion that all the reasons she left didn't matter. Laurel was here now. I lost my father. I found a sister I never knew I had. If I wanted a mother, I had to accept the one I had been given, faults and all.

None of us were perfect.

"You do?"

"Yeah, I do."

We separated, and Laurel smiled. She wiped away her tears and sniffled, retaking her seat.

"Would you like to look through the box?"

I did, but not right now. "I will. Later. I have something else in mind."

"Oh?"

"Lunch. Me, you, and Gail. My treat."

My sister winked. Laurel looked genuinely happy.

"Let's go." I held out my arms, and they each took one as we walked out of the apartment, toward the elevator, and hopefully into a fresh start.

LATER, AFTER LUNCH AND dropping off Laurel, I brought Gail back to The Roost and searched for Carrion.

He must have known I needed to talk to him. I found him in one of the family rooms. Alone.

When I entered, he glanced my way, gesturing to the table. "Care to share a beer, pres?"

"You knew I was coming." A beer sat at the empty spot across from him.

Carrion nodded.

I picked up the beer, popped the top, and chugged it. "You want another?"

"Yeah."

Good. I grabbed a six-pack and dropped it between us, dropping my ass into the seat. "Is it all true?"

"Would it make a difference if I said yes? Or no?"

It would. "You know it would."

"Then, yes. I visited Rook and told him everything. Laurel was there. It took some convincing, but when I showed them pictures of you as an adult, the club, and the future, they finally believed me and agreed."

"Doesn't that mess with some space-time continuum or some shit?"

He snorted. "I doubt it."

"You did this all for me."

Carrion sat back. "Yeah, I did."

"Why?" I held his stare, waiting for him to answer.

"Because you're the closest thing I've got to family, Crow. You're blood to me. You took me in, brought me into this brotherhood, and accepted me from the beginning. I had nothing before that."

"Damn, brother." I reached for my chest because the ache of those words felt like they would cave it in. "I love you, Carrion. I fucking do. You're like a blood brother to me, too. I can't ever thank you enough for this."

He shrugged. "I didn't do it for thanks."

I knew that. "You never do. You bear the burden of caring for every member of this club, searching through their lives for ways to protect them and make it better. You carry that burden because you want to, and that's fucking amazing. I don't say thank you enough, Carrion. You're irreplaceable. We wouldn't have the Devil's Murder without you."

"Fuck, Crow."

"I mean it."

"That's why I can't fucking breathe right now," he joked.

"C'mere, Carrion."

We both stood, and I brought him in for a hug. It wasn't much. A tiny gesture for all he'd done for me, but I hoped he felt how deeply I thanked him.

"You're not a ghost, and you're not invisible. You might move through the shadows and fly with the crows, but I see you, Carrion. We all do."

"Thanks."

"Now, let's stop hugging and start drinking. I need to know more about this ability of yours."

Carrion laughed. "It's gonna be a long night."

So be it.

Chapter 14

BELLA

"EVERYONE IS ACTING WEIRD," I confided to Bree. "They keep looking at me and smiling. It's fucking creepy."

Bree laughed. "Why? You don't want anyone to smile at you?"

"You know what I mean. Something is going on."

"I don't know what you're talking about." She shook her head and dropped cookie dough by scoop onto a baking sheet. "You're the president's ol' lady. Everyone loves you. So they smile. Big deal."

"Nope. I'm not buying it."

Bree shook her head. "You're crazy."

"I am, but this is different. You're baking a lot, too. I saw you cooking last night, and it looked like there was enough food to feed an army." My hands went to my hips. "Tell me what's going on."

"No."

There wasn't a second of hesitation.

"Bree."

"My lips are sealed."

Well, fuck. "I decided to change tactics. "I thought of a name for our shared business."

She popped the cookie sheet into the oven. "This should be good."

"It's amazing. I already created a logo and ordered business cards."

"You didn't." She frowned. "Tell me you didn't use Bling & Bake." She cringed.

"I'm insulted. This is perfect. You're going to love it."

"Alright. Tell me."

"Only after you confess what's going on."

"Bell, that's blackmail."

"Kinda. Oh, well. Cough up the goods. I need to know."

"No." Bree stared me down, and I could tell she wasn't going for it.

"Sis, please."

"Nope. You won't have long to find out, so live with it."

Fine. "You still want to know the name?"

"Of course."

"Sweet Sparkle."

She dropped the dishes in her hands, landing in the sink with a clatter. "Bella?"

"Yeah?" I asked, hopeful.

"It's fucking perfect."

Wow. My sister cursed. She must love it. Yes!

I reached into my pocket and pulled out one of the business cards to show her. I'd kept it since this morning when the rush order arrived from the printer.

"Here."

The card was pale pink and featured a dark pink slice of pie on a plate. The dessert sparkled with glitter. It sounded gaudy, but it wasn't. I thought it looked professional, simple, and unique.

Sweet Sparkle was embossed underneath the design. Under that, the words Treats & Bling. Yeah, I still found a way to get that word in there. Sue me.

"Oh, Bella." She ran her fingertips over the letters before tackling me in a hug. "You did good, sis. This is so amazing."

Yay!

"So we're doing this?"

She nodded. "Yeah. We're doing it."

I could hardly contain my excitement. I had to tell Crow.

Bree waved me off. "Go. I can tell you're too antsy to help me now."

She was right. I kissed her cheek. "Love ya, Bree."

"Right back at ya, Bel."

I raced from the kitchen and nearly ran into Lou. "Woah."

"Sorry."

"You're in a hurry."

"I've got good news."

"About?"

"I'm starting a business with Bree. Sweet Sparkle!"

Lou laughed. "I'll be your first customer."

"I'm holding you to that." I waved as I rushed to the bar.

Crow was seated next to Raven. He spotted me as soon as I entered. "Bella, baby. C'mere."

I didn't hesitate to jump into his lap. "You're never going to guess what happened."

He caught me and slid his arms around my waist. "Tell me."

"Bree said yes!"

"That's badass, babe. I'm thrilled for you."

"What did my woman agree to?" Raven asked with amusement.

"The Sweet Sparkle!"

He tilted his head to the side. "What's that?"

"Our bakery and bling shop."

Raven's lips twitched. "She needs that. Good." He finished his beer and pushed it aside. "I'll catch up with you later, pres. I need to go congratulate my woman."

Raven left us alone as I settled on Crow's lap.

Crow stood and placed my bottom on the bar. Strange.

He turned to the room. "Clear out!"

When the president gave an order like that, everyone obeyed. It took less than a minute to be alone.

"You have something to say?" I guessed.

"I do."

He cleared his throat and reached for me, planting my bottom on a nearby chair, moving me from the bar like he was nervous and couldn't decide what to do. "I don't want to wait." Crow dropped to one knee, reaching into his pocket. I didn't know what he meant until I saw the diamond ring. "Marry me, Bella, mine. This weekend. Saturday at sunset."

Oh. My. God.

"Austin," I whispered, unable to speak louder. "You want to marry me now?"

"I sure fucking do. I love you, Bella. There's no reason to wait."

"But there's so much to do. We can't pull this off in a couple of days."

"It's all done. Everything is arranged."

"Everything?" Damn. He was efficient.

Wait. That was all the secrecy going on around here—the reason for all the smiles. Everyone knew but me. My man was so sweet and sneaky.

"All but the dress. That's your part."

"I'll get one," I promised.

His lips claimed mine, nibbling on the bottom one before we separated. "I know you will, Bella, mine."

"Then, to clarify, yes. I'll marry you on Saturday."

Wow. Saying that aloud made me feel giddy.

"It's a date."

"YOU KNOW, YOU DIDN'T have to kidnap me for this," I laughed, clinking my wine glass to Bree's. She sipped on sparkling white grape juice instead of wine. Pregnancy prevented any indulgence until after the birth of her baby. Bree wasn't much of a drinker anyway. She didn't miss it.

"Sis, you're getting married tomorrow. You needed a girls' night before you tie yourself to Crow forever."

Forever. A simple but powerful word.

"Yeah, you're right."

It was hard to believe I was sitting on a couch wearing a fake diamond tiara on my head at my bachelorette party. A white sash draped across my torso, declaring me as THE BRIDE.

Cute. My sister didn't waste time picking these up.

"I still think we should have hired the strippers, Bree," Sadie cut in. "They had a guy who looks like that hot wrestler on TV. The one who has long hair and big muscles."

"That literally describes almost all of them," I laughed.

Sadie shrugged. "Yeah." She giggled before finishing off her juice—another pregnant woman who couldn't drink.

"Don't worry, Bella." Rebel dropped beside me on the couch in the private room we hijacked for the night. "I'll help you enjoy all the booze."

I still had no idea what she endured or lost at the hands of the vargulf. Now wasn't the time to bring it up. But I extended her an offer to stay at the clubhouse until she figured out her next move. For now, she accepted.

Snickering, I nodded. "Good. Callie is pregnant, too. You're all I've got."

Callie lifted her glass of sparkling red grape juice. "These men knock us up as soon as they get the chance, but I'm not complaining."

"Why would you? I've seen Hawk, Raven, and Crow. The whole club is full of hunky, protective, virile men. I'm jealous!"

"You never know," I joked, "maybe one of these bikers is your man."

She shook her head. "No, but I'll know him when I see him."

Sadie nodded. "Yeah, I think you will. I knew with Caden."

"I was so annoyed with Hawk, but I couldn't deny we had instant chemistry." Callie leaned back, rubbing her belly.

"Same," I laughed. "Crow is always cocky."

Bree reached for the bowl of chips and salsa. "I can't think about any of this while I'm hungry."

"We just had pizza."

"Sis, shush."

I refilled my glass with more wine. "When I'm pregnant, I bet Crow won't let me do a thing. He'll order me to put my feet up and treat me like a fine piece of china."

"There's worse that could happen," Rebel whispered.

Shit. I didn't think before I opened my big mouth.

"I know. Just ignore me. I have a disease."

She arched a blonde brow.

"It's called open mouth and insert foot disease, Bree clarified.

Laughter followed.

I glanced around the room at the women gathered and considered myself lucky and blessed to know each of them. I didn't know Rebel well yet, but I had an inkling that we would become close. She just had to let down her guard long enough to let me in.

Of course, I understood her reluctance. Trauma left ugly scars. They weren't always easy to forget and heal. I knew that from Bree.

Of the women we rescued, only Rebel remained with us.

I reached over and squeezed her hand. "You'll get through whatever it is. You're not alone."

She sighed. "We'll see about that."

Chapter 15

BELLA

"**I**T'S THE PERFECT DRESS." Bree smoothed the material around my hips, preventing any wrinkles. "The design is perfect for you, Bel."

I had chosen a mermaid style that hugged my figure, revealed enough cleavage to entice my new husband, and dipped low in the back—mostly silk with a bit of lace and pearls.

I couldn't agree more. Sadie, Bree, and Callie had spent the last three hours helping me with my hair and makeup. I'd chosen to pull part of it back and let the rest cascade over my shoulders in soft curls. Loose strands curled around my face. Bree had given me smoky eyes and glossy red lips.

"Here's something old," my sister announced, showing me the diamond tiara she'd worn to Homecoming her senior year in high school when she won and placed in the court.

"It's perfect."

She added it to the top of my head, arranging my hair so it fit without ruining the style, and pinned it in place.

"And I've got the blue." Callie held up earrings.

Diamond and sapphire dangles. "Ohhhhh, pretty."

I took them from her, slipping them in my ears.

Sadie grinned as I caught her stare. "I've got new and borrowed."

I wondered what could be both at the same time.

Sadie held up a bag. I snickered when I saw the label. "A garter. You have to return it later, so don't let Crow put his saliva all over it."

"No guarantees," I laughed.

"You're ready now." Bree stepped back to give me space. "Come look in the mirror."

I slowly rose and crossed the room to the full-length mirror Crow had bought me. Taking in my appearance, I had to blink back tears. "I don't think I've ever felt this beautiful in my life. Thank you."

All three girls rushed to me, and we hugged.

"I wish our parents were here, Bree."

"Maybe they are, Bel."

A knock at the door captured our attention. Sadie rushed to answer it.

"It's Lou!"

"Show him in." I turned toward the door, smiling as I saw how he'd cleaned up. "Handsome. I'm so lucky you're walking me down the aisle."

He grinned. "I can still walk. I just like to ram the tires of my scooter into all the members."

Soft laughter escaped my lips. "We're the best-lookin' people tonight."

He winked. "Don't I know it."

Lou had combed back and slicked his hair. He wore a dark suit and shiny black shoes, and I had never seen him dressed up before now.

He held out his arm. "Ready?"

"Yes."

Bree picked up my bouquet and pressed it into my hand. "I'm so happy for you."

"You're next."

"Maybe."

I took Lou's arm, and we left the room, anticipation and nerves almost getting the best of me.

Lou patted my arm. "You're fine. This is the man you love, and I'll tell ya a secret."

"Yes?" I asked, trying to ignore the fluttering in my belly.

"He's already confessed that you're his mate and the only woman he'll ever love, so there's nothin' to be nervous about."

Good point.

"But if he treats ya bad, I'll kick his ass."

I giggled.

"Lou."

"I mean it. Yer the closest I got to a daughter—you and Bree. You girls make me happy. I told ya this before, but I'm sayin' it again 'cause I love ya."

Awwww. "I love you, too, Lou."

When the music began, and I finally took that exciting walk down the aisle, I almost tripped on my heels. But then I spotted Crow, and everything seemed to snap into place.

I never had any doubts. Not one.

My only thought as I met his gray gaze was that I was the luckiest girl in the world. I was marrying a handsome biker bad boy who loved me as much as his club. I couldn't ask for more. God, the look he gave me nearly scorched my panties.

He wore a black button-down shirt underneath his cut and dark jeans, clean black boots, and a proud grin.

He had shaved his head and trimmed his beard. Everything about him looked shiny as a new penny. But the way his body filled out his clothes, damn, I got hot and bothered quick.

I never thought to ask him where we headed for our honeymoon, but I figured we were staying here and celebrating with our MC family. I ended up partially right about that.

As the years passed, I didn't think I'd remember what everyone wore or what they said at our wedding, but I would remember their faces and the way they made me feel—so loved. And boy, did everyone love Crow. He was a god among men, and in their world, he was royalty. It kind of made me the same now.

Hence, the tiara. A strategic addition by my sister.

When I reached Crow, Lou handed me off, but not without kissing my cheek first.

He turned to Crow as our hands clasped. "Treat her right, or I'll use my shotgun."

Half the guests laughed.

Lou took his seat, and the pastor began the ceremony. I couldn't focus on what he said, staring into silvery eyes that almost sparkled brighter than a star. Happiness and love poured from Crow into me. I didn't know we were exchanging vows until Crow spoke.

"I knew you were mine the first time we met. I promised myself I'd find a way to make you fall in love with me."

I had to smile at that. He was telling the truth.

"My whole life, I felt a little off, like I was missing something, but when I saw you, my Bella, it suddenly made sense. You were the missing piece."

Damn. I blinked to hold back tears.

"I'm gonna spend the rest of my days loving you and proving that marrying me was the best decision you ever made."

A few of the more vocal club members whistled and clapped.

I didn't know what I would say and didn't practice. I wanted it to come from my heart.

"Austin Derek Holmes, Jr, I noticed you the minute you walked into Bull's Saloon. I saw that sexy swagger and those stormy gray eyes, and I knew I would go anywhere you asked me to. It ended up taking only a few hours."

A couple of people laughed.

"I lost my heart to Crow, the president of the Devil's Murder, but it's the man I love. I promise to stand by your side, be your ride or die, and give you every piece of my heart because you already own it."

Crow clutched his chest. "Babe," he whispered.

"You're the real deal—a man of character. You lead, and I'll follow you anywhere. I love you."

I heard a few sniffles in the crowd but kept my focus on Crow.

The pastor said more words, and we exchanged rings, offering more promises. Then Crow gently slipped his hand around my back, tugging me against his chest.

"You're finally legally mine," he whispered before his mouth consumed mine, claiming my lips like my heart. That fucking kiss. Wow.

I felt almost dizzy when he finally leaned back, and the roar that followed was drowned by the look of adoration in his gaze. I'd never seen him look happier or more at peace.

"Now starts our forever," I murmured.

"Hell yeah, it does."

The receiving line lasted over two hours, and the photos took another hour. By the time we sat down for the night, my feet ached, my stomach rumbled, and I had never felt happier.

My sister had prepared a feast, and I ate next to Crow, sharing bites of food and stolen kisses. It was better than any fantasy.

When I was a young girl, I used to stare at the moon and wish for the man of my dreams to come and confess his undying love, carrying me off into the sunset. I had a better reality than that innocent daydream.

Crow held my hand and lifted it, dropping a kiss on top. "Have I told you yet how ravishing you look in that dress?"

"Nope. Describe ravishing."

"I'm gonna have to sit at this table all night, so I don't shock the guests."

"What if we snuck into a room, locked the door, and fucked like wild animals?"

He groaned. "Damn, Bella, baby. Are you trying to kill me on our wedding night?"

I laughed and shook my head. "No, but, uh, how about that room?"

No one said a word when we snuck off and got in our first quickie as husband and wife. I wondered if anyone heard me screaming his name because my man got me off so damn good that I almost saw stars. I told him he left me a present in my panties, and I would be wet all night. It must have driven him wild because he growled at my words.

We arrived back at the tent that had been set up for the festivities in time to share our first dance as a married couple. Crow spun me around as soft music played through the speakers, and I rested my head over his heart. I looked up once and found him staring down at me, a look so fierce I had to ask what was on his mind.

"I want kids, Bella."

Okay. "Now?"

"No," he replied, "but soon. Maybe a year or two. I don't want to be too old when they're teenagers."

"I'm fine with that."

"And I don't want to ever leave the club."

"Well, babe, I'm not asking you to do that."

"And I need you to stay with me forever, Bella, mine, because I can't imagine breathing without you by my side for a second."

Oh. Crow.

"I'm not going anywhere."

He nodded, hugging me close, and I felt him shudder.

"What's this about?"

"I just started thinking about our parents, how they would have loved to be here tonight, and how it scares the shit out of me to think we won't be together someday."

"Our lives and choices are different. We'll make it, Crow."

"I know we will."

"Then we're going to focus on each day as it dawns and try to make it better than the one before it. We do that; there's no regrets."

"None," he agreed.

"Then kiss me and seal the deal."

He didn't hesitate.

The Devil's Murder knew how to throw a party, and tonight was one of the most memorable. We danced and drank. We spent the night under the stars. So many people stood up and congratulated us that I switched out the champagne and wine for ice water. My cheeks hurt from all that smiling.

Laurel danced with Crow, and I swear it was a bittersweet but pivotal moment for my man.

I shared two dances with Lou.

When dawn came over the horizon, Crow scooped under my legs and headed toward our apartment.

I tried not to listen to all the suggestive and sexual descriptive comments that spilled from some of the guys. They had a lot to drink and meant well.

Crow carried me over the threshold and into our room, directly to our bed. He had me naked in less than a minute. "I think we better start practicing if we want those kids."

"Is that so?"

"Yeah. I need to feel your nails down my back. Hear those breathless moans in my ear. I need your body and mine fucking all night."

"It's daylight now," I teased.

"Okay. All fucking day."

"It's fucking day?"

He smirked. "Aren't all wedding nights and honeymoons designated fucking days?"

"You're right, babe. Give it to me good."

Oh, he did.

Epilogue

CROW

"IS THIS WHAT IT'S like to be married?" Bella asked, stifling a yawn with the back of her hand. "We haven't left this room in days."

Nope, we sure didn't.

"Keeping you between the sheets is the most fun I've had in years."

"Better than watching your enemy's soul reaped by a bunch of scary biker dudes dressed in black robes and carrying scythes?"

"Damn. That's a hard one," I joked.

Her fingers drifted across my face, stopping to tickle my beard. "You're a good man, Austin Derek Holmes, Jr. I don't know how I got so fucking lucky, but I did."

"Babe. Your sweet talk makes me fucking horny."

I wasn't kidding. My dick had seen so much action the last few days you'd think he would shrivel at the idea of being used again. Nope. Hard without much thought, I pressed my eager erection between Bella's thighs. And just like it had been for days, I slid into her wet, tight heat with a groan.

"The death of me, Bella, mine."

"Hmmm?"

"This pussy. You. Every inch of your sexy body. All these goddamn curves." I gripped her ass, pulling her onto me.

We shifted, and she straddled my hips.

"God. I don't think I'll ever get used to how you make me feel so full. You're so thick and long." She rocked her hips, gliding back and forth on my dick. "I love it."

I couldn't help releasing a groan. "Bella."

She pulled off me, dropping down to wrap her lips around my cock. Oh. Shit. I reached for the sheets, gripping the material in my fists as she began to bob her head. The suction of her hot mouth nearly did me in.

"I can taste us both," she informed me, licking the tip. "It's a turn-on."

"Babe, that's a new kink."

"Is it? Or maybe I just never told you how much I love to lick you and wrap my lips around this dick after you've been inside me."

I reached for her hair, tugging her head back. "How the fuck are you so perfect? Because now I need to shove my cock in your pussy until you scream."

"What are you waiting for?"

I had her on all fours, knees, and palms flat on the mattress when I began pumping into her hard from behind. That naughty talk from her pouty pink lips sure fired me up. Lust fogged my brain. I couldn't stop rutting into my woman.

Wait. Not just my woman. My *wife*.

"Fucking love you, babe."

"You better. The way we're going at it, you're going to knock me up." She turned to look over her shoulder at me. "Do you think you can come so hard it spills out, and you have to shove it back inside me?"

Where the fuck was this coming from? A dirty book? She loved to read what she called smut.

"Babe. Have you been getting ideas from your books?"

She wasn't offended. "I take inspiration from everything. Books. Movies. Porn when I masturbate and think of you."

"You're not gonna have much time for the last one."

"I sure hope not."

Goddamn. I gripped her hips harder, slamming into my ol' lady, my wife, and the reason I fucking breathed. She was going to take this dick and love every minute.

Married life was even better than I imagined.

HERON

I SHUT DOWN THE engine on my bike, lifting off the seat to secure my helmet before walking toward the entrance to The Roost. After my initial meeting with Crow, I felt something shift inside me, an invisible thread pulling tight to connect me to my brethren. Crows. Just like me.

Fuck. I didn't think I'd ever find anyone who understood my bond with the black-feathered bird. I searched for years to find anyone who experienced what I did.

As an adopted child, I discovered early on that I was different from my parents. They didn't speak to the crows as I did. They didn't understand why the sky would fill with layers of onyx wings that followed me wherever I went. Or why I felt their emotions and connected on a spiritual level, sharing their feelings.

I could count on the crows. They never left me.

But now I needed to learn more about the bond I shared with them and how I became a crow-bonded male. It wasn't like I could go to the local library to study or search on the internet to find the origins of my species. Shifters and soul-bonds weren't common. I needed answers, and Crow promised to provide them.

I just had to agree to prospect for their club. One year. An agreement that would change my life. I didn't hesitate to accept.

Now, I stood on the precipice of change, ready to embrace whatever fate led me to this moment. I still had so many questions. Would I locate my birth parents? Every attempt to find information about them had failed. Why did they give me up? Did Crow and his club know of other groups like this one? Were there communities out there that existed apart from society so they could thrive without human interference?

It made sense. But I wasn't going to learn much until I gained the club's trust. I had to prove my loyalty, and in return, Crow pledged to help in any way he could.

I wasn't left with many choices after my adoptive parents died. Rebellion, loss, and anger brought me to this moment.

The door opened in front of me, and I stopped, sucking in a breath as I stared at the girl in front of me. I'd seen her face a hundred times before now but never met her until this moment. A stranger from my dreams, I glimpsed her nearly every night in the last six months.

She was more stunning in person than I could have imagined.

Ruby red lips. High cheekbones dusted with a light dash of pink. Eyes so fucking blue they reminded me of a cloudless summer sky. Long blonde hair braided on both sides of her head rested over her breasts. Curvy. Tanned, bare legs that I couldn't wait to touch to see if they felt as smooth as they looked. And that smile. Words didn't do it justice.

Fucking hell. She was goddamn gorgeous.

She popped a hip, placing her hand on the indentation at her waist. "Are you gonna stare at me all day, crow boy?"

Crow boy. I almost laughed. How fucking ridiculous and true.

"No," I managed to reply, "but since I like what I see, I just might consider it."

Her brows lifted. I caught her by surprise.

"Who are you? One of those Devil's Murder bikers?"

Not yet, but I would be. "In a year. I'm a new prospect."

She snorted. "What are you considering?"

"Right now?" I answered truthfully. "You, baby."

"Oh, I don't date bad boys."

Yeah, she did. Little liar. I watched her tongue flick out and lick her bottom lip. She sized me up and didn't appear disappointed. Good.

"I'm not a bad boy, remember? You said so a minute ago. I'm a crow boy."

Her lips twitched. "I guess I did."

"What's your name, spark?"

"Spark?"

"I'll explain in a minute. Your name," I repeated.

"Rebecca, but I go by Rebel."

Rebel. It suited her.

"What's yours?"

"Heron."

She blinked. "That's unique. Why did you call me spark?"

"You remind me of my favorite pepper."

She squinted before huffing, tossing her long blonde braids over her shoulders. "You're comparing me to a damn food item."

"Yeah, 'cause you're a little sweet and a whole lot of hellfire."

Rebel snorted. "That's the worst pickup line in existence."

"That's why I just spoke the truth instead of trying to impress you."

"You're too cocky."

"Never heard any complaints before now, darlin'."

Rebel poked a finger in my chest. "Stay away from me."

"You know that won't happen."

"If I say so, it will."

"Alright. Your choice."

She grinned in triumph.

"I won't be going anywhere, Spark." I picked up her hand and kissed her palm before releasing it. "We both feel it."

She opened her mouth to argue but closed it with a snap.

Yeah, I thought so.

If you're curious, you might have guessed that the storyline for the vargulf is a twist on Beauty and the Beast. Sadie is Caden's Belle. I had a lot of fun writing it. It's always been one of my favorite fairy tales.

The next book in the Devil's Murder series, *Heron*, will release March 2025.

Cuckoo will release in June 2025.

Want more Undertaker/Caden?

He's got a new club name, and more adventure awaits.

Stay tuned for the **Night Striders MC**.

Book #1 is *Rebel Road*, anticipated release summer 2025.

Watch for more in the **Devil's Murder MC** series.

You can read more about Grim and his club in the Royal Bastards MC Tonopah, NV Chapter, now available.

Find all Nikki's Royal Bastards MC and Devil's Murder MC books on Amazon and Kindle Unlimited.

Never miss out on a book! Follow Nikki on social media to receive updates.

Love motorcycle romance?

Check out these books by Nikki Landis:

Royal Bastards MC Tonopah, NV

#1 The Biker's Gift

#2 Bloody Mine

#3 Ridin' for Hell

#4 Devil's Ride

#5 Hell's Fury

#6 Grave Mistake

#7 Papa Noel

#8 The Biker's Wish

#9 Eternally Mine

#10 Twisted Devil

#11 Violent Bones

#12 Haunting Chaos

#13 Santa Biker

#14 Viciously Mine

#15 Jigsaw's Blayde

#16 Spook's Possession

#17 Infinitely Mine

#18 Grim Justice

#19 A Crossroads Christmas

#20 Sinfully Mine

#21 TBD

Royal Bastards MC Las Vegas, NV

#1 Hell on Wheels

#2 Reckless Mayhem (Manic Parts 1 & 2)

#3 Jeepers Creepers

#4 Rattlin' Bones

Mayhem Makers: Manic Mayhem (Manic Part 1)

Reaper's Vale MC/Royal Bastards MC Crossover

#1 Twisted Iron

#2 Savage Iron

Feral Rebels MC/Royal Bastards MC Crossover

#1 Claimed by the Bikers

#2 One Night with the Bikers

#3 Snowed In with the Bikers

Kings of Anarchy MC Ohio
#1 Property of Scythe

#2 Property of Mountain

#3 TBD

Summit Hill Vipers
#1 My Stepbrother Biker

#2 My Tattooed Hitchhiker

#3 My Ex-Boyfriend Stalker

#4 My Hero Biker

#5 TBD

Mayhem Makers: My Inked Neighbor

Saint's Outlaws MC
Prequel: My Christmas Biker

#1 Brick's Redemption

#2 TBD

Ravage Riders MC

#1 Sins of the Father

#2 Sinners & Saints

#3 Sin's Betrayal

#4 Life of Sin

#5 Born Sinner

Night Striders MC

#1 Rebel Road

#2 Ravaged Road

#3 Vengeful Road

Iron Renegades MC

#1 Roulette Run

#2 Jester's Ride

#3 Surviving Saw

Origins: Ground Zero

Pres/Founder – Crow

VP/Founder – Raven

SGT at Arms – Hawk

Enforcer – Talon

Secretary – Carrion

Treasurer – Claw

Road Captain – Swift

Tail Gunner – Jay

Member/Tech – Eagle Eye

Member/Cleaner – Cuckoo

Member/Healer – Falcon

Member – Heron

Prospect – Goose

Prospect – Robin

Playlist

Heartbeat Failing – Dead By April

BLACK SOUL – Shinedown

Trigger – Smash Into Pieces

Karma Kills – Through Fire

Halo – Savage Hands

Vengeance – Zack Hemsey

No Apologies – Papa Roach

Werewolf – Motionless In White

THE WEIGHT OF IT ALL – Smith & Myers

Animals (Abbey Road Version) – Architects

Run – Plush

Narcotic – Bryce Savage

STILL CHOSE YOU (feat. Mustard) – The Kid LAROI

Werewolf (feat. Bring Me The Horizon) – Lil Uzi Vert

I Am The Lightning – Des Rocs

AFRAID TO DIE (feat. Tatiana Shmayluk) – P.O.D.

On My Way (Marry Me) – Jennifer Lopez

You can find Nikki's Playlists on Spotify

SNEAK PEEK
MY
STEPBROTHER
BIKER

GAGE

I DIDN'T LIE WHEN I told Letty on the night of the wedding that I'd be seeing her around, but I also didn't confide that she wouldn't be having any contact with me during those two years.

And now, after the long wait, I finally had permission to reappear in her life.

My right knee wouldn't stop bouncing as I tapped my thigh, eager for church to end. Storm sent me a look as he noticed, and it distracted him. Shit. I crossed my arms over my chest and leaned back, stretching out my legs under the table in the center of the room. The club's logo stretched across the surface, etched into the wood. The same emblem I wore on the back of my cut.

I prospected for this club in high school and patched in the summer after I graduated. The men gathered around this table were family. Not a soul related to me by blood. That didn't matter in my world. We were brothers, bonded through our allegiance to the club and our way of life.

A concept my father would never understand. The only thing he recognized was dollar signs.

I focused on Storm's words, refusing to steal a glance at my phone to check the time.

"Boomer, Wolf, get your asses to that meeting. We need eyes and ears on that shit. Don't get seen and cock it up."

They nodded, rising from the table to head out.

Blendcore Enterprises, my father's company, merged corporations and sold goods and companies, whatever they could get their greedy hands on. Lately, that included weapons that supplied our enemies. We needed more intel and the only way to get it included spying on meetings between our rival club and the mediator from Blendcore.

"You sure that dancer from Show 'N' Tail got the info right?" Cash asked, flicking ash from his cigarette onto a tray. "Ain't doubting your word, pres. Just lookin' out."

Storm grunted. "Yeah, she's good for it. No love for the fuckers at Blendcore. They bought out the company that owned her apartment building and had her evicted."

Damn. "Fuck," I cursed, shaking my head. I hated hearing this shit. My father was ruthless, and his reputation was confirmed every time we learned something new.

"This ain't on you, Blade," Storm reminded me. "We've been over this shit."

Yeah, I knew. "I still don't like it."

Cash gripped my shoulder, giving it a shake. "He's his own man, just like you. Let it roll off."

He was right. I nodded, giving Storm an anxious look.

"Church is dismissed. Get the fuck out of here," Storm ordered. His gaze fixed on me as I stood. "Blade," he growled.

"Yeah, pres?" I asked, anxious as fuck to get out the door.

"I know what these last two years cost you. It didn't escape my notice."

I dipped my chin, acknowledging his words.

"Not been easy for you, son, but things are about to change. Keep Letty safe. Whatever, however."

Wow. I slapped my hand over my chest. "Thank you, pres."

"You understand why I had to do it, right?"

His order. The one that kept me from the girl I loved for two fucking years. The agony of it burned in my gut.

"I see you, Blade. I fucking know it hurt, but she was sixteen. Fucking *sixteen*, and you were almost nineteen. Had to keep you clear of that shit."

"I know." I hated it. I would have been with her the whole time. Would that have placed her in additional danger? I couldn't say. My protection never wavered. From the moment I left that wedding, I kept an eye on Letty. If I wasn't around, I asked another prospect. She never went without me or one of my guys. No one fucked with my girl.

And no one *fucked* my girl. I made sure of that.

"I hear you, pres."

Cash sighed. "The shit with her mom and your dad, it had to stay clear from both of you. It was necessary."

"Yeah." They weren't wrong, but I wish I could have explained before I walked away. I left Letty with vague comments and a promise she didn't understand.

And then, this morning, our rival threatened Mifflin and his family. The Crimson Heretics felt cheated by Mifflin's latest deal, pinching off a considerable percentage of their profits. Pissed, their president sent two of his men, who gunned down Mifflin's secretary and left him a package that included her severed hand and a warning. A photo of Cynthia and Letty splashed with blood.

How did we know?

Because Candy Cane, the stripper from Show 'N' Tail, had a magical pussy that seemed to keep Mifflin addicted. He liked to talk to her, thinking she kept his secrets. She never did.

Funny enough, Candy Cane had a thing for Storm. Whatever he wanted, she did. Only with Storm, she knew better than ever to try to betray him.

So, here I stood, waiting for permission to get to my girl. Sure, a prospect arrived at the high school stadium in case shit went down before I could come, but I hated the delay.

"Pres," I pleaded.

He ticked his chin toward the door. "Go. You keep me informed. Got it?"

"Yeah, pres!" I shouted, running out of the goddamn door like my ass was on fire.

Just the idea of being close to Letty again, speaking to her, and breathing the same fucking air pulsed a need in me so fucking deep that I didn't know how I would stay in control once I had a chance to touch her. The ride on my Harley took fifteen minutes. Way too fucking long.

I almost missed her fucking graduation. I arrived in time to see her step onto the stage, relieved to confirm she was alive, unharmed, and as beautiful as ever.

"Leticia Marie Jacobs."

Her name was announced, and she glided across that stage with a smile so fucking huge I clutched my chest to ensure my heart still beat inside it. I waited at the bottom of the stairs, knowing she had to exit where I stood.

She didn't see me at first, but when we touched, she fucking felt the connection. Her head snapped to the side, and her lips parted. Shock flittered over her features.

That's right, baby. I'm back.

Nothing would tear us apart again.

I couldn't keep my hands off her, holding her hand because I needed that contact. I had to feel the warmth and breathe in her sweet scent. My thumb caressed her skin for the remainder of the graduation ceremony. Once it ended, we stood as Cynthia congratulated her daughter.

My focus turned to the mother. Would she stay with Letty and out of trouble?

She slid her gaze across mine, meeting long enough for me to understand that she had to leave. Cynthia hid the shit with Mifflin from her daughter for two years. She tried to protect her and failed. My father only cared about himself. She learned that lesson far too late.

There wasn't a soul he wouldn't sacrifice to stay at the top. That included his wife, son, and stepdaughter.

After we stopped inside the school and the girls picked up their belongings, we walked to the parking lot.

"You're with me," I announced to Letty. "Come on, Beautiful. I'll follow Ava."

I led her toward the black Mustang I borrowed for the day, leaving my bike for the prospect. He'd ride it back to the clubhouse. Tomorrow, I'd switch them out for my bike.

Her eyes widened when she saw the car. "You have a Mustang?"

"Tonight I do."

She stared, unmoving.

"Love, I knew you'd be in a dress and heels. Not exactly the right clothes to ride me."

She arched a brow, caught my meaning, and blushed as pink colored her cheeks. "Ride your bike, you mean."

"Right."

I opened the door, devouring every inch of skin she exposed, and shut it once she had buckled her seatbelt. "What are your plans tonight?" I asked to make conversation once we left the lot.

"Parties." She shrugged. "Probably a lot of them."

Yeah, I figured. I did the same when I graduated, only instead of getting my dick wet, I spent the night wishing she was with me and getting drunk off my ass.

She wouldn't be drinking that much on my watch.

151

The dinner bored me. My attention kept drifting to Letty's toned, silky legs, and I couldn't keep my hands to myself. I slid my palm over one thigh, hiding my movements underneath the tablecloth. We sat with our backs to the wall, pushed in close enough that no one would see unless they ducked under.

With slow, careful caresses, I rubbed circles over her bare flesh, kneading the soft skin.

Her lips parted, and she tried to pry my hand off, only to find I wouldn't budge.

She was a temptation I couldn't indulge in for so long that now I had no way to fight it. All the time apart increased my need and spiked my lust and desire to new heights, the denial sparking a possessive, obsessive drive that could only be tamed by making her mine. In every fucking way.

"Gage," she whispered, trying to keep the moan out of her voice.

"Yeah, Beautiful?" I asked, sliding my hand to the right, reaching the edge of her panties.

"You can't," she began, gripping the arm of the chair when I slid a finger beneath the fabric, teasing the seam of her slit, daring to push through and find the slick proof of her arousal.

"I can," I growled as I leaned down, whispering into her ear. The loud restaurant blocked us from being heard. "I need a taste."

I pulled my hand back, lifting it without brushing her skin, and went straight to my mouth, sucking on the finger as she stared.

Her pupils blew wide. Lust darkened the shade of blue in her eyes until I stared into sparkling sapphires. *So fucking gorgeous.* I needed to wake up every fucking day to those pretty eyes and that tempting mouth.

"So fucking good," I told her, swirling my tongue before pulling my finger from my mouth, lowering my hand, subtly making my way across her thigh.

This time, she opened wider, letting me have better access.

"So impatient," I murmured, kissing the pulse point below her ear. "Do you think they'll notice when I make you come?"

She gasped. "Gage."

"The taste of you, Beautiful. It's burned into my brain. I can't function without it."

Her legs closed so fast I nearly growled. "And yet you stayed away."

She shoved my hand to the side, and I let her.

"This conversation isn't over, baby." I sat back, picked up my drink, and drained the cup.

"What if I say it is?"

Oh, Beautiful, this isn't a game, but if you want to play, I'll win.

I captured her hand, lifted it above the table, and pressed my lips to the surface, stroking once with my tongue. "Challenge accepted, Beautiful."

Her hand pulled away, but not before I caught the hunger she tried to hide.

Tonight, one way or another, we were hashing this out, preferably with my tongue or lips on her body.

***My Stepbrother Biker*, Summit Hill Vipers** releases
April 2025.

SNEAK PEEK

My BREATH SHUDDERED THROUGH my chest, my lungs dragging in gasps of air as if they couldn't entirely fill right. Blood pounded in my ears and roared through the canals as my hands shook, still gripping the baseball bat in my hands. Slick crimson fluid coated the wood, staining it bright red.

"Rowen."

Everything felt surreal, as if I watched from afar, outside of my body, so disconnected from reality that I wasn't sure if oxygen made its way into my lungs or not. My mind felt fractured, disassociating from the carnage and the man sprawled on the carpet only a few feet from where I stood. I could see the bruise forming on his forehead and the bump swelling from where the bat made contact. I'd hit him. Twice.

"Rowen," Kate emphasized with a wince as she wrapped an arm around her waist. "Babe. Give me the bat."

I blinked, slowly moving my head to turn in her direction.

"That's right. Hand over the bat."

I released a shaky breath but didn't move.

"Honey, he can't hurt me right now." She groaned as she tried to reach out, and I fell to my knees, releasing the bat as I dropped it next to her side.

Her hand fell to her lap, lying limp from a dislocated shoulder. The left side drooped at an awkward angle. It had to hurt like a motherfucker.

A sob escaped, but I felt more building within the cavern of my chest, ready to burst free and tear me apart from the inside out.

"Rowen. Look at me."

I lifted my head, trembling as I made eye contact with my best friend. "Kate."

"There you are," she whispered with a nod. "Good. Listen, I need to call 9-1-1. You can't be here when the police arrive."

Shit.

"You've got little Jacob to think of. He can't lose his mama."

"I know," I croaked, clutching my bloody, shaking fingers in my lap. "I almost killed him."

"But you didn't," she reminded me, "and if you had, it would have been self-defense."

Yeah, maybe. Would the police see it that way?

"You're hurt," I blubbered, fighting back tears. My eyes stung with the effort.

"But I'm alive. You saved me, Rowen." She unwrapped her torso, and I grasped the hand that extended toward me, holding it as tightly as I could without causing further pain.

"I'd do it again."

"I know, babe. That's why I love you."

Kate's boyfriend, Jack, nearly killed her. If I hadn't arrived when I did and found his hands around her throat, she might not be breathing right now.

I saw the bat leaning against the wall and picked it up, swinging before I could think through what the hell I was doing. I just had to get him off her.

I should have been there sooner, but Jacob wanted to show me one of his drawings, and I couldn't leave before he finished explaining about it. When I let myself inside Kate's house, I found her locked in a struggle with Jack. He'd already beat on her long before I arrived.

Even now, I could see her lip swelling and the crusted, dried blood on the corner of her mouth. The bruise on her jawline. One eye was swelling shut and discolored. Both were bloodshot. Dark handprints stood out on the tan skin of her neck, already changing color and darkening the longer she sat and leaned against the wall.

Jesus. Why did abusers always find and prey on the weak?

"You need a doctor," I sniffled, close to losing my shit.

"I'll get one, Rowen. Jack is going to go away a long time for this. They have to arrest him this time." She squeezed my hand and released it. "Go wash up in my bathroom and rinse the blood off, then get to Jacob."

We heard motorcycles outside, and I froze.

"Someone else is here."

Jack the Dagger, known by his associates as Dag, didn't belong to a motorcycle club, but he ran within that circle and knew other hitmen, guns for hire like him, with even less morality. If they saw me, I would be taken and questioned, beaten, and possibly killed for my involvement.

"Call 9-1-1. Now," I ordered, rising to my feet. "I won't abandon you. I can't."

She hissed as she tried to get up, and her ribs protested. A soft cry left her busted lips. "This isn't your fight. It's mine. You've done enough, Rowen. Get the hell out of here. Go out the basement door and through the back gate. They'll never know anyone else was here."

"Kate," I pleaded.

She knew we had no time to argue. And she knew the one and only reason I would abandon my best friend. "Imagine Jacob's face when you don't come home."

I stopped breathing with such an image in my head. Failing my son wasn't an option.

Guilt, already riddling through me, my eyes locked on the door where other men would soon enter the house. What would happen when they saw Jack on the ground and injured?

"Look at me." Kate swiped across the screen as we heard voices outside. "I'm getting help." She dialed 9-1-1. "Go."

In slow motion, I watched her lips move, speak into the phone.

In slow motion, I felt my legs lift me from her side.

"I love you," I told her before the pure love for my son had me running down the hall, through the kitchen, and opening the basement door. I slipped through the opening and shut it behind me with a soft click, descending the stairs as quickly and quietly as possible. All the while, my mind begging emergency services to arrive in seconds, hoping there wouldn't be a delay.

Since I had been in this house numerous times, I knew where to walk without bumping into anything, and I found the stairs in the dark that led to the exterior door. My heart hammered inside my chest as I rushed, desperate to get home to my son. Right before I opened it, I heard two gunshots.

My hand slapped over my mouth in horror as I stumbled, feeling every bone in my body shudder with shock. Humid exhales pelted my trembling palm as I stared to where I'd just come, praying to hear her voice as a sign she was still alive.

But her voice was gone. The only ones I heard now were angry as the door opened at the top of the stairs. One of them belonged to Kevin Keeler, Jack's best friend. His reputation with knives terrified me. Kate had told me some frightening stories. He was heading this way!

"She wasn't alone, you stupid fucker. Didn't you see the shoe print? Someone else was here."

The hand not covering my mouth reached behind me, blindly searching for a doorknob. My only chance of escape. Again, I froze when hearing sirens. The wail grew louder as they sped toward us. The 9-1-1 operator must have heard the shots fired.

An order was barked. "Whoever is down there, I want them dead. And their fucking family."

It was eerie to know help was arriving, yet they couldn't save me. These kind of men didn't play by rules not their own.

My body flooded with adrenaline and the protective instinct a mother carried for her child. I quickly chose flight mode for survival. I snuck outside, stayed close to the fence, and ran toward home. I didn't stop until I reached the house I rented, grateful I didn't drive the short distance since I had wanted the exercise.

Without a car at Kate's house, maybe they'd never figure out it was me who had been there. Swallowing sobs for my friend, I rushed to the hose in the backyard and rinsed the blood off my hands. When I finished, I hurried around the front, careful to ensure no one followed. I sprinted inside and shut the door, panting as I leaned against the wood and struggled to calm down enough to focus.

"You okay, Rowen?"

I jumped.

My babysitter sat with her textbooks on her lap, studying when I barged in.

Already trying to cover any trail of where I'd been, I replied, "Sure," far too clipped. "Just decided to, uh, run tonight, but, ummm, I got a cramp." I cringed with the lie, but Tina didn't know where I went. I hadn't told her.

She closed the textbook and yawned. "I need a break. Good timing."

Hoping my nervousness wasn't noticed, I watched her pack up her stuff and I handed Tina forty dollars for the few hours she was here. I pretended to be casual. "Thanks. I hope Jacob behaved."

"He always does. He's the sweetest boy."

"He is," I agreed, and needing to sound normal even thought my heart felt like it would crash through my chest, I asked, "Umm, did he go to bed okay?"

"We read four stories first." She laughed. "He loves superheroes."

Jacob didn't just love them. He was obsessed. . . and now I needed one.

I walked the babysitter to the door and watched her climb into her dark blue clunker and drive away. Before shutting the door, I scanned both sides of the street—no other cars. No people. Nothing suspicious.

I took a slight sigh of relief until an image pelted my mind. It was of Jack waking up, pissed, telling his biker friends it *was me* who hit him!

The brief calm was now drowning in more panic. Jacob and I couldn't stay here. It wasn't safe. Jack's companions would want to silence me about Kate.

I had to run and get as far from Palmdale, California, as I could. I didn't have much money, but I would drive until the funds gave out. At some point, I would stop at an ATM and withdraw every bit of cash my limit allowed.

To pack in lightning speed, I pulled every curtain and twisted the rod on all the blinds closed in every window. The place was sealed tight. I left a light on in the living room, one above the stove in the kitchen, and my bedroom.

My thoughts scattered as I refused to dwell on Kate.

I couldn't do a damn thing to help her now.

My focus had to remain on Jacob and sneaking away before Jack and his friends showed up on my doorstep.

It didn't take long to pack a couple of suitcases, even though it felt like eternity, every sound making me a nervous wreck.

I brought all the essentials and the few sentimental items I owned that I could never leave behind, like Jacob's scrapbook of his first year and the framed photo of my parents. I packed two big bags for Jacob and an old diaper bag full of treats and toys.

Everything I owned that meant anything to me went into my car inside the garage. I loaded it with a cooler and drinks, some bags of groceries, and the big carry-on bag I picked up last month with all of our stuff from the bathroom.

I managed to fit everything inside and surveyed the house, giving it a final check to be sure I left nothing behind. Furniture and plants could be replaced. Those things weren't necessary right now.

I crept into my son's room, wanting to watch him sleep as I always did, but his life was on the line. He turned six last week, and I couldn't believe how fast he'd grown. He was sharp, too. He was way more intelligent than the average child, or maybe I just thought of him that way. He spoke with a maturity rare in kids his age.

Trying not to wake him with fright, I sat on the edge of his bed as the light spilled into his room from the hall and brushed the dark hair back from his forehead. "Jacob."

He mumbled in his sleep but didn't rouse.

"Jakey, baby. I need you to wake up for a minute."

"Tonopah," he mumbled, blinking.

"What?"

"Tonopah. That's where we're going." He opened his eyes and pointed to the drawing on his nightstand.

I followed his gaze to the sheet of paper with a fresh drawing he'd made tonight. Me, Jacob, our car full of boxes and bags, and a sign that read TONOPAH.

I didn't even know where that city was located.

California? Nevada? I never heard of it.

"Don't worry, Mama. I know where we're goin'."

He climbed into my lap and reached for his drawing, holding it to his chest.

"We have to go now."

I didn't ask how he knew. I never did.

My son drew things on paper that most would never believe. But they were always correct. If Jacob saw Tonopah, I was supposed to go there. I'd use GPS once we left town.

I buckled Jacob into his highbacked booster seat and covered him with his Superman blanket. He hugged his stuffed Batman to his chest and gave me a sleepy smile. "I'll put this drawing with the rest."

He nodded as he yawned. His eyes fluttered.

I didn't check the other drawings in his backpack, but I knew they held more secrets, more hints about our future. I didn't have the time to look at them now.

Urgency pushed me to sweep the house one last time, taking any other artwork of Jacob's, his Hot Wheels cars, and the last few things I missed. When I had it all in the car, I closed up the house, locked it, and took my place behind the wheel.

I glanced in the rearview mirror, swallowing as I watched him sleep. No one ever explained how parenthood would change my life.

Once you had a child, your life took a backseat to the precious one entrusted to you. I would sacrifice anything for my son.

The love I felt for him surpassed any love I'd ever experienced. More than my parents or my brother. Deeper than my ex-boyfriend. A parent's love for a child was more profound, selfless, and life-changing than any other on this earth.

I would fight for Jacob until I no longer had life in my body. I wondered, even then, if I would defend him from beyond the grave.

"I love you, my beautiful boy," I whispered, merging onto the street as I left my driveway.

I caught the garage door as it closed in my rearview mirror and hoped that I would leave danger behind in California without dragging it behind us, kicking and screaming, into our new life.

Infinitely Mine is available to read now!

ABOUT THE AUTHOR

Nikki Landis is a romance enthusiast, tea addict, and book hoarder. She's the USA Today Bestselling Author of over seventy novels, including her widely popular Tonopah, NV RBMC series. She writes wickedly fierce, spicy romances featuring dirty talkin' bikers, deadly, possessive reapers, wild bad boys, and the feisty, independent women they love. Nikki loves to write character-driven, emotionally raw stories where protective, morally gray anti-heroes fall hard for their ride-or-die.

She's a mom to six sons, two of whom are Marines. Books are her favorite escape. Nikki also writes steamy alien and monster romance under the pen name Synna Star. She lives in Ohio with her husband, boys, and a little Yorkie who really runs the whole house.